Under One Sky

Time Travel Guardian Romance Series, Book 1

Zoe Matthews

Contents

Chapter One

June, 2017

Destiny Goodman pulled out her key and used it to open the door to the gallery she worked in. After closing it behind her, she relocked it and walked to the back of the store, depositing her personal belongings on the desk she was assigned to. She immediately went to the small room where new deliveries were kept until they could be unpacked. A grin grew wide on her face when she saw the boxes she had been waiting for sitting in a corner. She quickly checked to see if her boss, Aurora Callaghan, had come in, but her office was empty. Shrugging her shoulders, Destiny picked up her water bottle and filled it with ice and water. Walking to the boxes that needed to be unpacked, she set her water bottle aside and opened the first box.

"Oh, how beautiful," Destiny breathed with delight as she pulled the first item out. It was a lovely Native-American pot.

Destiny worked in a small store called the *Majestic Art Gallery*. The gallery featured many local artists, along with others who were willing to ship their creations to them. The *Majestic Art Gallery* had been in Aurora's family for many years, passed down from father to son for many generations. Aurora was the only child of her parents, so she was able to inherit it. It was very well known and popular among the local people of Denver, Colorado, and had grown to a national level as well. Artists all over requested that Aurora represent them, and they had a large waiting list. In fact, Aurora was considering moving to a larger building, even though the *Majestic Art Gallery* had been at the same location since the late 1800s.

Destiny held the pottery out in front of her, admiring it at all angles. She ran a finger lightly over the colorful painted design and smooth clay. She picked up another vase and walked into the main room where most of the items were displayed. The pottery and vases looked like what someone might find in an ancient Indian site, even though they were just recently created. They were hand-made, and the details of the designs were painted with precision. She placed the pottery on the shelf where they belonged under the artist's name. As she continued to empty boxes, she found herself thinking about her life.

She had been born in Albuquerque, New Mexico, and her childhood hadn't been a happy one, mainly because she had been born with an odd gift. She had a strong ability to know and understand people's emotions and feelings, which she now knew was called empathy. She could touch someone and immediately know what they were feeling about whatever they were thinking about.

Destiny's gift had scared her parents. She couldn't count how many times they had taken her to a counselor or psychologist in order to "fix" her. She had been put on so many different types of medications, she'd lost count. As she grew older, she eventually learned to hide and suppress her gift. She pretended she was "cured" and lied whenever her parents asked her if she could still read other people's feelings. But she had to stop touching people because when she did, her gift kicked into high gear.

She remembered an especially emotional time when her best friend in high school had come to her very upset, confessing that she was pregnant. When Destiny put an arm around her friend in comfort, she immediately knew her friend had become pregnant because of a date rape. She had felt all of her friend's emotions and hurt, along with intense fear. The feelings that had radiated from her friend were very strong, and they had scared Destiny. Since her friend hadn't volunteered the information that she had been raped, Destiny hadn't dared to let her know that she somehow *knew*, and she had kept quiet, supporting her the best that she knew how as a sixteen-year-old girl through words of comfort.

But after that experience, she did everything she could to suppress her gift. Whenever she felt an emotion from another person, she learned how to shut it down. Eventually it had become second nature to her to automatically block other people's feelings and emotions. She didn't want to know what other people were going through or feeling. She just wanted to be normal like everyone else.

When she was a teenager, she took an art-history class in school and fell in love with art. She talked her parents into letting her take painting classes. She just knew she would someday be a famous artist with paintings in high demand. But sadly, she was never any good, but she did her best to develop her interest. When she went to college, she decided to major in art, but after a few years of taking classes, she finally realized she didn't have a talent in creating art. After finally admitting this to herself, she switched her major from art to business management. If she couldn't create art, she could at least surround herself with it by eventually owning her own gallery.

Right after she graduated from college, she applied for a job at the *Majestic Art Gallery*. For some reason, the instant Aurora had met her, she hired her without even an interview. One of her art teachers who had known Aurora had given Destiny a reference for the job. After Aurora read the letter, she had asked Destiny a few questions about the classes that she had taken and made sure she was willing to work the hours needed. After giving Destiny a short tour of the gallery, she had been hired.

As Destiny placed the last vase on the shelf, she glanced at a small room that was located off the side of the main-display room that Aurora used to use for storage. A few months ago, Aurora informed her that she was planning on turning the room into a place dedicated to the past and to deceased artists whose work had been forgotten, although she wasn't planning on selling any of the items. The room would be used kind of like a museum. Their customers could not only enjoy browsing in the *Majestic Art Gallery* until they found the perfect item for their home or a gift, but they could also enjoy seeing forgotten art.

Some of the art wasn't very good, in Destiny's opinion. There were a few paintings that looked like a child had painted them, but Aurora displayed them because they had been completed over one hundred years ago. Maybe that style had been popular during the 1800s, Destiny finally concluded to herself after studying some of them. Of course, she had studied that era in some of her art classes, but some of the styles Aurora displayed were very different than what she had learned about. There were also some cracked pots that were most likely from ancient civilizations, and some colorful Native-American blankets pinned to one wall that Aurora claimed one of her ancestors had created.

There was one specific painting that fascinated Destiny. In the center on the largest wall was a beautiful depiction of a small dainty cottage, one that someone might find in a village in England. It had a thatched roof, and the cottage had red trim around it. There were large full trees nearby, and it almost looked like the branches were trying to protect the little cottage. Beautiful gardens of flowers surrounded it with a stone path that led towards a stormy sea in the distance.

The artist's name was Clara Moore, although Destiny could barely read the signature, because it was so faded. To Destiny, it was one of the most beautiful paintings she had ever seen. There was something strange about it, though. When she stood just a little to the right of the cottage, it was almost as if the painting came alive. She could almost smell the fragrance of the flowers in the garden and the salt in the air from the nearby sea. If she moved away from the painting, the sensations and smells diminished. She never said anything to Aurora, chalking it up to her weird childhood gift.

Destiny heard the back door of the art gallery open and knew that Aurora had arrived. She pulled her cell phone out of her pocket and saw that it was almost time to open the gallery. Turning her back on the painting, she walked to the back room to let Aurora know she was working on unpacking all of the boxes that had been delivered.

"Hello, dear," Aurora greeted her when Destiny entered her office.

"Hi," Destiny responded. "I was able to put all of Devin Booth's pottery on her display."

"That's great," Aurora said with a smile.

Destiny watched as the older woman took off a gray sweater. Even though it was June, Aurora seemed to always have that particular sweater with her, rain or shine. Destiny studied Aurora for a moment. She couldn't say she was very close to Aurora, but she did enjoy being around her. Destiny didn't know how old she was, although if she were to guess, Aurora would be in her early to mid-40s. Aurora wore her hair long, keeping it in two loose ponytails that covered her ears. She always wore long, flowing, colorful skirts. Destiny decided once that Aurora would have fit in perfectly with the Hippie Era in the 1960s.

"We are supposed to get a shipment from Tom Grant today," Aurora commented, as she swept out of her office into the main room to unlock the front door.

"That's good," Destiny responded. "I had noticed that his display is getting low."

"When it comes, if we aren't too busy, I'd like you to restock his shelves."

"Alright," Destiny agreed happily.

She loved it when Aurora let her put the various artist's work on the shelves and walls. It was her favorite part of her job. When Destiny had first started working at the gallery, Aurora had done that job all by herself, but after a few months she had let Destiny begin to stock a few shelves. Now, Aurora let her stock more and more of the different artists' work. There were now only a few that Aurora insisted she do herself. Destiny loved to touch each piece, wondering why the artist had made it, the history behind it. If she allowed herself, she could use her gift to answer those questions, but she never did. She only allowed herself to feel the peace and creativity the artist had felt as they had created it.

The moment the door was unlocked, a woman and her small daughter walked in. It was time to start the day.

Chapter Two

*J*une, 2045

It was late afternoon, and Graham Dawson sat at his desk, finishing up the last of the paperwork to his latest assignment. It had been a standard job and one of the easiest he had worked. He had only been gone a few days this time, even though his boss, Jack McGee, had told him it might take a week. Graham was hoping that, after he finished the paperwork, he would be able to take the next day off, since technically he was supposed to still be gone anyway.

He had been working for *Shadow Works Detective Agency* for five years now. The company's main focus was finding individuals that had become lost during *The Terrible War* and helping people fill in their ancestral lineage. It had become more and more common for people to come to them, wanting to know what happened to their relatives during the war, even though it had officially ended over fifteen years ago. Quite a few of their clients wanted their genealogy sheets to go as far back as possible. It was becoming the norm for people to want to know where they had come from, who their relatives were and what happened to them.

A few years ago, his boss, Jack McGee, had added a new division to the detective agency which few people actually knew anything about. Graham was one of a handful of employees that Jack had asked to work in the new department, which Jack had named the *Time Travel Agency*. Graham's new position was now called a *Time-Travel Guardian*.

His new responsibilities were to travel around the world using a fancy, time-travel watch that Jack had designed to find, collect, and bring back time-travel devices or shut down any portals they found. Sometimes he was able to do his job in his own time period, but most of the time, he had to travel to other eras and countries to do his job.

Not wanting to think about that awful war in United States history and why he even had the job he had, he quickly finished the last paper and signed his name. Gathering up all the papers, he slipped them into the file, ready to be given to his secretary to process.

He leaned back in his comfortable chair, and closed his eyes, allowing himself to relax for a moment. His phone vibrated, and he sighed to himself as he pushed the accept button, instantly seeing that it was Jack.

"I need to see you ASAP," Jack said without giving a greeting.

Graham could see his boss on the small visible screen that appeared just above his phone and noted that his emerald eyes were twinkling.

"Another job?" Graham asked, trying to keep his voice steady.

"When can you get here?" Jack asked instead of answering Graham's question.

Yep, Jack had a new job for him. "I'll leave as soon as I can." Graham signed off the call and picked up the file he had just finished, resigned that he probably wasn't going to get any time off.

Jack's office was located in the building next to his. He quickly decided he would walk there instead of taking the driverless car that was always at his disposal. He needed the exercise and also needed to think. He did his best thinking as he walked.

As he prepared to leave the building, he was waylaid by his secretary who wanted in-structions about some work he had given her the morning before he had left for his last job. Another woman wanted to know when a certain project would be completed, and a third flirted with him as she hinted that she'd love to meet him for dinner. He easily dismissed the attention of the third woman and, although he was always friendly with her, he did his best to not encourage anything. He glanced down the hall at an empty office, wondering when the occupant would be back. The owner of the office was Trystan, his younger brother, who was very likely on his own time-traveling job.

After he talked to the women who were demanding his attention, he was finally out the door and heading towards Jack's building nearby. Jack's office was in the largest building in the *Shadow Works Compound*. He operated and ran the entire complex and, even though he was in his early fifties, he continued to work full time. His knowledge of how to find people and the history of the world was vast. If Jack didn't know something, he knew how to find the information, and find it quickly. When the general public needed *Shadow Works* services, it was this building they were directed to. Few people were allowed in the building next door, the building where Graham's office was located and where the *Time Travel Agency* operated. This was where all the *Time-Travel Guardians* worked.

As Graham walked, he allowed himself to think about why he was even working for *Shadow Works* in the first place, and he had to go back about twenty years ago, when he was fifteen years old. War broke out all over the world in 2025. In history books it was called *World War III*, but everyone who survived called it *The Terrible War*. His only concerns when he was fifteen were basketball and whether his team was going to make state finals, and a girl named Ellen who was in his fifth period math class.

When war started between a few countries in Europe, he remembered hearing his parents talking about it, but no one was very concerned that it would affect them in America. But only six months later, United States was pulled into the war. A few months after that, the war became personal. America was attacked, and life for Graham was never the same again. In fact, life had changed for every American. After the war ended three years later, there were quite a few children left without parents, and many orphanages had opened up to accommodate them. Most of them were now adults, and slowly the orphanages were being closed.

When the war was finally over in 2028, almost half of the world's population had been killed in some way: whether it was by bombs and guns, disease and plagues, or starvation. Graham was eighteen by that time, and he had lost his parents and two sisters. He was left only with his younger brother, Trystan. Everyone he knew had lost at least someone in the war, and most lost quite a few people. A number of his high school friends hadn't made it.

Graham hated to think about that time, but sometimes he couldn't help it. His life would never be the same because of that war. After the war ended, everyone who was left started to rebuild the cities that were destroyed. The United States economy had totally collapsed during the war, and so everyone started over in the same boat. There were no longer people who were rich and had a lot of money or belongings. Everyone had lost almost everything. Even though this was very difficult for some people to grasp, Graham felt that it was a blessing in disguise. It allowed everyone to start over on the same page. He was grateful that the United States had been saved and that they were still the same country, a land that he loved.

A few years after the war ended, most people were starting to feel comfortable again. They had jobs and food on their plates. Schools were opened for the children. Then people started to wonder what happened to some of their relatives. A couple who lived in California had had relatives who had lived in New York just before *The Terrible War* started. What happened to them? Where were they living now, if they were still alive? And *Shadow Works Detective Agency* was born. Jack McGee had a talent for finding people using current technology. At first he had worked by himself, but he soon became so busy that he started to hire people to help. Graham and Trystan were some of his first employees. Over the next few years the company grew until over one hundred people worked for them. The company became very good at finding out what happened to people. Some people even hired the company to do full genealogy sheets for them. A great interest had developed among many people to want to know where they came from, even if it meant they would have to go back several generations.

After the company had been in business for about five years, Jack started to see some strange things in a few people's lines. There would be holes in the line where there shouldn't be. It was like that person had just disappeared. Other times, a person would appear in a family line with no history of when or where he or she had been born. He started to research as to why this was happening. That was when Jack figured out that time travel was causing these holes, or breaches as he sometimes called them.

Over many months, Jack finally discovered that just before the year 2000, many people were worried that a huge catastrophe was going to happen, because most of the computers they used at that time weren't made to go beyond 1999. Some people thought everything was going to shut down the instant time shifted to January 1, 2000. It was called Y2K. Nothing happened, at least that people knew about. But something did happen deep in the earth. Many devices and places all over the world became activated for time travel. Jack could never figure out why or how those devices could suddenly be used for time travel; it had just happened.

At first people discovered these by accident. Someone would wear a very old necklace and be transported back in time. They were either able to return to their time or they weren't. It all depended on what device was used and where it went. These trips caused the holes. At first Jack had thought it was really neat. He'd always believed in time travel and his favorite book was *The Time Machine* by HG Wells. He loved the idea of time travel, and Graham knew that once Jack figured out how some of the devices worked, he even used them a few times himself. But then he realized that around 2015, people were starting to believe time travel was real, that it wasn't fiction. And there were people who started to search for the devices. Some of these people were able to find them and not only to use them to go back in time, but to also go forward, into Jack's future. This especially happened during the war by people who wanted to escape the horrors of it. History was being changed, and that was not good.

Armed with all of this information, Jack went to a friend who worked with the US government. Eventually a secret agency was formed, and headquarters was part of *Shadow Works*. Most of the *Shadow Works'* employees didn't know about the Time Travel part of things. The main part of the business still helped people with their genealogy. But when a hole in a person's line was found, it was flagged. If it was determined that the hole was caused by time travel, Jack called in the *Time-Travel Guardians*. Graham was one of them, and his job was simple.

Travel to whatever time period he needed to, using a device Jack had invented called the Ziran Watch.

Find the time-travel device.

Confiscate it by purchasing it if the owners agree. If they don't, figure out a way to remove it without them knowing.

Bring it back to 2045.

Turn it over to Jack, who in turn turned it over to government authorities. Usually the device was stored in a large warehouse which was located on *Shadow Works'* property until the government officials decided what to do with it. Graham knew that usually the devices stayed in the warehouse indefinitely.

End of job.

Usually, once a job ended, Graham worked on the regular genealogy and detective jobs until he was called into Jack's office again. He hardly ever communicated with Jack unless there was a time-travel job, so Graham knew that he would be leaving again soon. Part of him was excited about the prospect of a new job, since he loved Time Travel and visiting new eras and new places, but he also wanted some time off.

The distance between the two buildings took about ten minutes to walk, and soon he was taking the elevator up to the top floor where Jack's suites were located. After identifying himself to the building operator, the door opened, and Graham stepped inside.

Jack's office was decorated by the best technology available. Since the war, technology had taken off, and they were now more advanced than they ever were. Things were constantly being developed and invented and improved. Jack took advantage of every new technology available to him.

But surprisingly, Jack's office also was decorated in a fantasy-type theme. Small fairy and leprechaun statues sat on shelves around the room. Paintings hung on the walls that depicted fairy houses and other worldly images. It was like Jack liked what the modern world could offer him, but he also liked the simplicity of what used to be and of where his ancestors were from, Ireland.

Graham was aware that Jack was of Irish descent, so he figured that was why there were fairies and leprechauns around. In fact, Jack had a set of clothes that he sometimes wore when he went on his own time-travel jobs that made him look like a funny leprechaun: black pants, white-pressed shirt, shiny black shoes, green-velvet vest and a black-top hat with a four-leaf clover tucked in the brim. Jack's full head of hair had turned pure white in his advanced age that completed the Irish leprechaun look. To Graham, Jack looked older than his age of early fifties because of his white hair.

Jack was as eccentric as a man could be, but he was also smart as a tack and still able to run a large company like *Shadow Works* at his age. Graham had nothing but respect for this man who had taken a chance on him and his brother, Trystan, by giving them a good job after the war had ended even though neither of them had had any experience in detective work.

"Hello, Graham," Jack greeted him with a large grin, a firm handshake and then waved to a nearby chair.

Graham returned the greeting, instantly being able to tell that his boss was unusually excited about this particular job.

"Sit down. Would you like a drink?" Jack offered.

Graham hesitated and then shook his head. He knew that, if he accepted a drink, Jack wouldn't tell him anything until his drink was gone, and he wanted to know what was making his boss so excited.

"Good, good," Jack sat down next to him, his green eyes dancing. "I know that you just returned from a job. Great work by the way."

"It was pretty easy to get the necklace. The owner wasn't very careful about keeping it hidden. I found it on her dresser," Graham explained, although he knew Jack would be reading his full report that gave detailed events that had happened.

"Glad that it went so well and that you were able to return with it so quickly. I have just discovered a painting," Jack said all in the same breath.

Graham was used to Jack jumping quickly from one subject to another. He sat back against the comfortable couch, waiting for him to continue, knowing that eventually he would have all the information.

"I need you to retrieve it. But this time, the painting needs to be delivered here, to my office. I don't want it taken to the government building for storage until I see it."

"Okay," Graham said slowly when it was obvious that Jack wasn't going to continue. "Can I ask why you need it to be brought to you?"

"You will know the reason when you see the painting," Jack replied.

Graham sighed, although he was also used to Jack only giving him bare necessities about each job. Jack expected him to read the file and research the information on his own. "Okay. Give me the particulars. I will leave in the morning." He hoped the job was going to be fast like his last one.

"You will be traveling to 2017. The painting is located in a shop called the *Majestic Art Gallery*. It should be an easy recovery. At the moment, it is supposed to be hanging on a wall in a small room. I think the owner will be willing to part with it, but if not, just wait until the room is empty, and then bring it here."

"Sounds easy enough," Graham commented. "What is so special about this painting?"

"I'm actually not quite sure how it activates time travel, but it's a *Clara Moore* painting."

Graham perked up at Jack's words. Clara Moore was an artist of the late 1800s whose paintings only became priceless about fifty years after her death. She had created many different paintings and hadn't sold or displayed any of them. After her death, they were stored in an attic of the small house she had grown up in for years until a relative sold the cottage that included the entire contents. The new owner discovered them and hung a few in the cottage, thinking they were amateur paintings and not worth anything. Eventually a new owner turned the cottage into a bed and breakfast, and a famous painter who spent a few days there became fascinated by them. He offered to purchase them, and the owner allowed him to buy all of the paintings that weren't being displayed in the cottage. Over many years the paintings were shipped all over the world, and they became priceless. But Graham had never heard that they were connected to time travel.

Jack handed him a thin file. "All of the information you will need is here. Your watch is still working correctly?"

Jack asked this question at the beginning of every job.

"Like a dream."

"Good, good," Jack murmured, as he stared off into space.

Graham stayed silent, used to the man's quiet musings. As he waited, he was tempted to open the file, but he refrained, and decided to read through it when he was alone.

After a few minutes, Jack's body jerked, and he looked at Graham as if surprised he was still there. "Please keep me appraised on your progress."

Graham nodded his head. "I'll let you know when I am on my way. It shouldn't take more than a few days. I would like to request a few days off when I return."

"Sure, sure," Jack agreed. "You've been working hard. You deserve some time off."

Graham stood. "I'll be on my way then."

After goodbyes were said, Graham was soon on his way out of the building. This time he ordered a driverless car and directed it to take him to his own apartment which was located few miles away. When the car stopped in front of his large apartment complex, he gave new information to the car and watched it as it pulled into traffic and drove away, heading towards the *Shadow Work's* garage. After he entered the complex, he skipped the elevator and took the stairs two at a time to the third floor. Once he entered his apartment, he dropped the file on his coffee table. He opened a nearby cupboard and took out some fish food.

A large saltwater aquarium took up almost an entire wall of his small living room. It was full of colorful fish. He'd wanted to get a pet when he first moved into this apartment, but he was gone too much to take care of one, so his compromise was keeping fish. They only needed to be fed twice a day, but it didn't matter if he was an hour or two late. When he went on trips, he made arrangements with a young boy who lived down the hall to feed his fish for him.

He sprinkled food on top of the water and then spent a few minutes watching the fish. He had two types of angelfish, some clownfish, gobies, and a few algae-eater fish. He went into the kitchen, pulled out a reheatable meal from his freezer and heated it up. He ate while he looked over the file. Sure enough, there wasn't very much information in the file. The most important information was the exact time, date, and place he was to travel. He would import this information into his Ziran watch just before he left. The rest of what was in the file Jack had already told him.

Graham pushed his meal away, debating what to do next. Part of him wanted to leave in the morning. He could relax, spend the evening watching a new movie on his screenless television and eat a huge bowl of buttered popcorn. But he knew if he left now, he might be back the next morning, and then after delivering the painting to Jack, he could take a week's vacation. Maybe he could see if Trystan wanted to go with him to the cabin their family had owned before *The Terrible War*. It would be fun to spend time with his brother for a few days. They could do some fishing in the river that ran nearby the cabin and go on a few hikes.

Finally making a decision, Graham decided to leave that evening. He went into his bedroom and pulled out his small backpack that he always took with him on his time travel trips. It was full of emergency supplies, a change of clothing, three days of ready-to-eat meals, and a few bottles of water. He had a closet full of clothes of different time periods that he could wear so he wouldn't be out of place in the time period he was traveling to. He didn't have to make very many adjustments, because he was only going back to 2017. He also made sure he had the currency for 2017, along with the cards they had used back then to purchase things. He was hoping the owner of the gallery would be willing to let him purchase the painting and immediately take it with him.

There was one main rule he absolutely had to follow when wearing the watch. He was to never take it off for any reason once the watch was activated. If he did, it would immediately stop working, and he wouldn't be able to return home to 2045. This was an easy rule to follow since the watch was fused around his wrist. He was unable to take it off unless he deactivated it. It didn't have straps, just an ancient leather-looking band where the ends were fused together. It didn't look like the watches that were now being developed. To another person who didn't know what it was, it just looked like an old-fashioned watch from the late 1800s or early 1900s. But when Graham touched a button on the back of it, the watch instantly converted to a time-travel device. He was able to use it to travel to any time period he wished, to any location he wished. It had an emergency button that he could push to instantly transport him back to his apartment in case he was in a situation he needed to get out of quickly. Its battery was solar operated. It would last for weeks, but when he needed to charge the battery, all he needed to do was allow the sun to shine on it for a few seconds.

The last thing he did was put the information in the watch for the gallery he was heading to in 2017. Then he slipped on a jacket, his backpack, and then covered his hand over the entire watch face. He felt a vibration that started light, but grew stronger and stronger until he faded and disappeared.

Chapter Three

*J**une, 2017*

"You can go to lunch," Aurora told Destiny, as she glanced at a large clock that hung above the checkout counter.

"Great," Destiny responded with a smile. "I think I'll eat at the cafe today. Would you like me to bring you back something?"

Aurora nodded. "The usual, please."

Destiny grabbed her small bag and hurried out the door. The cafe she wanted to eat at was only a few doors down from the *Majestic Art Gallery*, and she ate there almost every day. Once she was in the cafe, she stood in line for a few minutes before ordering sandwiches and drinks for both Aurora and her. At the last minute, she added two chocolate-chip cookies. Aurora usually didn't want dessert, but Destiny figured that if the older woman didn't want her cookie, she'd eat both of them. After paying for the food, she left the cafe, deciding to eat her sandwich at her small desk. Then she would take a walk to the nearby park for some exercise.

As she left the cafe, she ran into what felt like a huge boulder. The drinks she held fell to the ground along with the bag of food. Soda pop spilled all over the place, but the bag stayed sealed.

"Oomph," Destiny groaned in pain.

"I'm soooo sorry," the boulder said, as he took her arms in order to help her stay upright.

"It's... it's okay," Destiny tried to say.

"I wasn't expecting the door to open like that."

Destiny's vision began to clear, and she looked up at the most attractive man she had ever seen. He was a good six inches taller than she was with sandy hair that curled at the tips. His blue eyes sparkled at her in concern and a tingle traveled from where he had grabbed her arms. He had a backpack on and a jacket, even though it was quite warm. She took a careful step back, effectively breaking contact with him.

"Are you okay?"

"Yes," Destiny told him as she bent to pick up the sack of food. "The drinks aren't though."

"Let me replace them for you."

"You don't need to do that," Destiny protested. "It was partly my fault. I was in a hurry."

"I insist."

Destiny bent down and picked up the empty cups. After throwing them in a nearby trash can, the man gestured with his hand and then opened the cafe door. Destiny hesitated and then entered the restaurant. The man followed behind her. The line wasn't as long this time, and Destiny was quickly able to reorder the drinks. The man stepped forward when the cashier told her the amount owed. He pulled a credit card out of a leather wallet and paid for the drinks. Very quickly, they were standing outside the cafe again.

"Thank you," Destiny said with a bit of embarrassment.

They both looked at each other. It seemed as if time stood still for a moment before the man answered. "Again, I'm sorry I ran into you."

The man gave her a half-bow and then disappeared back into the cafe. Destiny sighed. As she walked back to the gallery, she tried not to think about the tingle that went through her entire body when the man grabbed her arms to keep her from falling. She had never felt that type of sensation before when touching someone. What did it mean? She entered the gallery and walked to the back room and to her desk, nodding to Aurora in greeting because she was helping a customer.

Destiny sat down behind her desk and started to eat her sandwich. While she ate, she did her best to forget what happened. Whatever that tingle meant, she knew she would likely never see the man again. She pulled her tablet out of her bag and brought up the current eBook she was reading. She started to do what she did every work day at this time. She lost herself in a story.

Graham went into the cafe and stood at one of the large windows, watching carefully as the woman he had just run into entered a nearby business. He quickly glanced at the sign that hung above the building and read *Majestic Art Gallery*, and his heart clenched. The woman had gone into the gallery where the painting was. She most likely worked there since most people didn't take food into an art gallery unless they planned to eat it in a back room.

He debated what he should do. Part of him wanted to go inside the gallery, find the painting, and disappear with it, but his gut feeling was telling him to wait. He gave a sigh before turning away from the window and walked to the counter. He ordered his own sandwich and drink, relishing that he would be able to enjoy a cola. Soft drinks weren't very accessible in 2045 since most people felt they weren't healthy and refused to drink them. But he remembered how good a cool cola was from his childhood, and he was eager to taste it again.

He sat at a small round table and enjoyed his dinner. While he ate, he pulled out a small tablet and wrote down his plans. He would spend the night somewhere in 2017. He would go to the gallery when it opened in the morning and collect it. If all went according to plan, he would be back in 2045 by lunchtime the next day.

After he threw away his trash, he left the cafe. He decided to wander around Denver for a few hours. One of the things that he enjoyed in his time-travel jobs was to explore the time period he was visiting in. He had been all over, including the early 1900s, the 1500s, and one time he had even gone to 1292. He had also been all over the world in his own time. He enjoyed visiting, but he was very careful to talk or communicate to as few people as possible. One thing that Jack had talked about extensively during Graham's training was to be very careful to not change history.

One of the things he was amazed about Denver in 2017 was the amount of people there were. He actually started to feel claustrophobic with all the people that were on the sidewalks, each in a hurry to go wherever they were heading. Driverless cars hadn't been invented yet, and there were tons of vehicles on the roads. He even witnessed a small accident, something that rarely ever happened in his time since the driverless cars were programmed to be able to avoid crashes. He watched with a short laugh as both owners of the cars got out and started yelling at each other as to who was at fault. Graham left when a police car pulled up behind one of the dented cars.

When the sun started to set, Graham decided he had better find a place to sleep for the night. He followed directions on his watch to a nearby park and was happy to find a perfect place to spend the night, although he wasn't sure how much sleep he was going to get. The park had many full-grown trees. There was a pine tree where its branches almost touched the ground, a perfect place to hide. He used the park's restroom and then crawled under the tree. He pulled a solar blanket from his backpack and spread it out on the ground. He laid on the blanket, glad that it was summer. He hadn't come prepared to sleep in cold weather.

He made himself comfortable and started to think over the events of the day. His thoughts brought him to the woman. Every child that was born since the end of *The Terrible War* was born with some type of gift. Even though he was born in the year 2010, he had been born with the gift of empathy. When he had grabbed the young woman's arms after running into her, he felt all sorts of emotions from her. There was bafflement, shock, pain, fear, and then… attraction before he was able to block her feelings. He admitted to himself that he had also felt a connection to her.

"It's a good thing I'm leaving tomorrow," he muttered to himself.

He hadn't been interested in dating for quite awhile. His entire focus had been on his job. In order to do it well, he needed to make sure he didn't have any distractions. But he definitely couldn't be attracted to a woman, not in his time period. It also puzzled him. In all of his travels to other eras, he'd never had a reaction as he'd just had, and he didn't even know her name.

The next morning he woke when the sun started to rise, surprised that he had slept so well. He stayed under the tree until his watch read that it was eight o'clock. To pass the time, he ate one of his ready to eat meals. Then he pulled out his notebook and made notes of what he did the day before and his plans for that morning.

Soon he was walking out of the park and down the street towards the gallery. He knew it likely wasn't opened yet, but he wanted to be around when it did. He was anxious to finish this job and start his vacation. If all worked out well, he'd be home by lunchtime.

Chapter Four

At exactly ten o'clock, Aurora opened the front door to the gallery. Destiny noted that there were a few people waiting to come inside. She was working on arranging a new display for an artist, but she raised her eyebrows at Aurora, silently asking her if she needed help. After seeing the slight shake of Aurora's head, Destiny turned her attention back to her job.

A few minutes later, the door opened again, and Destiny saw the man who had run into her the day before, walk in. He immediately started to look around, and Destiny couldn't take her eyes off of him. His clothes looked slightly wrinkled and dirty, and she noticed he was wearing the same jacket and shirt that he'd had on the day before. She hardly had time to consider why, she was too focused on the small smile he gave Aurora. He held himself very confidently, and she fought the urge to approach him, since she knew Aurora would let her know if she needed help. Aurora said something to the man, and he shook his head, pointing at the Navajo blanket he was looking at, and Destiny knew he was telling her he just wanted to look around.

She turned her attention back to the display, but she kept track of the man out of the corner of her eye. Suddenly, she felt a presence behind her.

"Well, hello," the man greeted her, amusement in his voice. "We meet again."

Destiny turned around as her heart skipped a beat. What was going on inside her every time she was around this man?

"Hi. Welcome to *Majestic Art Gallery*. Did you find anything that interested you?" Destiny asked, doing her best to keep her voice professional.

"We might as well introduce ourselves. I'm Graham Dawson."

"I'm Destiny," she said, being careful not to say her last name.

Graham held out his hand to shake, but Destiny took a step back. The last thing she wanted to do was to touch him. She didn't like all the confusing sensations she had felt the day before, or what she was feeling right then for that matter.

"Can I help you find something?" She quickly glanced around the gallery, and she didn't see Aurora anywhere. The few customers that had entered the gallery were gone, and Destiny assumed Aurora had gone back to her office to do paperwork like she did every morning.

"I'm looking for a specific painting. Do you have any others than what are displayed in this room?"

Destiny hesitated. "We do have some in that room over there, but they aren't for sale."

"Can I see them anyway?" Graham asked with interest.

Destiny shrugged her shoulders and led him to the room. Once inside, she watched as Graham stood before each painting, studied it for a few moments before moving on to the next one. When he saw the painting of the cottage, he stopped and looked at it with great interest.

"I can't believe you have a *Clara Moore* painting," Graham said with delight.

"Do you know her work?"

"Yes, she's quite famous where I come from." Graham turned to her. "Are you sure this isn't for sale?"

Destiny nodded. "None of these paintings in this room are for sale. They are collections that my boss owns. She is displaying them here so others can enjoy them."

Graham didn't say anything, but Destiny noted a flicker in his eyes before turning to study the painting again. She moved beside him, at the moment forgetting about her vow to stay away from him.

"I love this painting. But there is something weird about it," she told him.

"Really? What's so weird about it?" he asked curiously.

She hesitated, almost wishing she hadn't said anything. From previous encounters with people, she had learned to keep any strange thoughts or feelings to herself. Why would he be any different? But for some reason, she couldn't stop herself from talking. "When I stand in a certain spot, it's almost as if I can smell the flowers and the salt from the sea."

She watched his face carefully for the usual patronizing look she would have received from others, but he continued to look at her as if interested in what she was saying.

"Where is it that you stand?"

Destiny moved to the exact spot. Instantly, she could smell the garden. She could almost swear she felt some water splash on her face. She glanced at the ocean behind the cottage and then gasped in shock.

"What is it?" Graham asked.

"I know this might sound strange, but I could have sworn that hawk in the sky was on the right side of the painting. Now it's on the left." She glanced at him quickly and moved away from the painting. "I'm being silly. Obviously, I am remembering it wrong."

But she was absolutely sure she remembered where the hawk was originally, because when she first saw the painting, she found it odd that there was a hawk near the ocean. Her only experience of seeing hawks was in the nearby Rocky Mountains.

"Perhaps," Graham said as he stood in the exact spot she had stood in.

Destiny wanted to ask him if he could smell the flowers like she had been able to, but she didn't dare. She watched him for a few long minutes as he stared at the painting in silence. When she felt they had been in the room long enough, she started to suggest they leave, but then he turned to her. Again, Destiny noted something strange in his eyes. What was making him so different than any other man she had met before?

"Are you sure I can't talk your boss into selling? I could pay more than it's worth."

"I guess you could try," Destiny shrugged.

Turning to the painting again, she suddenly felt a strong desire to touch it, which was strange. She was always very careful to not touch any art unless she had a specific reason to do so. She reached her hand out to touch the door of the cottage.

The instant her fingers touched the painting, she heard Graham yell, "No! Don't touch it!"

Destiny heard Graham shout, but before she could move her hand away, she felt a strange sensation. The room seemed to vibrate, slight at first and then became stronger. Her surroundings started to fade around her. She felt very dizzy and covered her face with her hands, willing the swirling to stop, and after a few moments it did. When she felt she could stand without falling over, she dropped her hands to her side and looked around in shock. She was no longer in the art gallery. Instead she was standing on a well-kept stone path that led to a cottage a short distance away.

"What happened?" she muttered to herself, as she took in her surroundings. "Where am I?"

The cottage looked exactly like the one in the painting she had touched just moments before. There were beautiful flower gardens all around the cottage. A large shade tree covered a section of the garden, and a small wooden bench was tucked beneath it, inviting anyone who wished to sit and relax for awhile. She could hear ocean waves in the distance and even saw a hawk soaring in the sky.

"This is very strange. I must be dreaming."

A faint humming drifted on the wind which made Destiny pull her attention away from the hawk. It sounded like someone was singing. Following the sound, she slowly walked around the cottage and saw an older woman bending over some flowers. She was humming a song Destiny wasn't familiar with. The woman was small and looked to be in her late forties or early fifties. She had on a faded, flowered dress that hung to her ankles and strange-looking shoes. She had brown hair streaked with gray that was braided and then rolled into a bun at the nape of her neck. She had a knife in her hand which she used to cut a few daisies and set them in a basket near her feet before moving on to cut some other flowers. A bee buzzed near her face, and she waved it away before continuing her chore.

The woman must have suddenly sensed that she was no longer alone among her flowers for she straightened and turned around. For a moment they both stared at each other; then the older woman grinned.

"Well, now. Welcome. Where did you come from?"

Destiny didn't answer for she had no idea what was going on or what to tell her. She started to feel panicked, but she quickly shoved those feelings away, knowing that there must be a perfectly logical explanation. The woman set down the small knife she was using in the basket and walked toward her.

"I am Mrs. Clara Moore," the woman said, introducing herself.

"I'm Destiny Goodman. It's nice to meet you," Destiny said politely. The woman's name sounded familiar to her, but her head was still swirling too much to place where she had heard it before.

Mrs. Moore looked up at the sun. "It's almost time for my morning tea. Would you like to join me?"

Destiny wanted to decline. She didn't make it a habit of joining strange women for tea. She actually wanted to look around and get her bearings. Her stomach growled painfully, and she found herself accepting the invitation.

"That would be nice," she agreed reluctantly.

"Come inside then," Clara invited with a wave of her hand.

Destiny followed her towards the small cottage. It had a thatched roof that looked sturdy and red trim around the white-brick exterior. A stone path led right up to the front door with a variety of colorful flowers bordering it. As she looked around, she suddenly realized that the cottage looked just like the one in the painting. The trees looked the same, along with the gardens that surrounded the small home, although some of the flowers were of a different variety. She couldn't see the sea that was in the painting, but she could hear the surf in the distance.

For a moment she felt numb. What had just happened? It was almost like when she had touched the painting, had she somehow been transported into it? But that didn't make sense. That was impossible...wasn't it?

"Your gardens are lovely," she commented to Clara, as she sniffed the flowers, recognizing the same fragrance she could smell when she stood in that specific spot in the gallery.

"Thank you, my dear. They are my pride and joy," Mrs. Moore said with a regal nod.

The older woman opened the door and allowed Destiny to proceed inside. She led Destiny through a very small living room and into an even smaller kitchen. She bustled around, setting a tea kettle on the cast-iron wood-burning stove, and then pulled out two cups and saucers from a cupboard.

"Can I help you with anything?" Destiny offered, although she didn't know what she would have helped with since she'd never cooked anything on a wood-burning stove before.

Mrs. Moore declined, so Destiny sat at the kitchen table, trying not to stare at the kitchen. She felt like she had fallen into another dimension or world. There weren't any modern appliances. Not even a fridge. It seemed that Mrs. Moore did all of her cooking on the old-fashioned stove. She couldn't see a microwave, coffee maker or other such appliances that were common in most modern kitchens. The floor was made of wood slats that were swept clean. Colorful braided rugs covered different parts of the floor.

After Mrs. Moore poured the tea and offered Destiny some cookies, although the older woman called them biscuits, they were both quiet for a few minutes.

"You seem to be a long way from home," Mrs. Moore finally broke the silence. "Where are you from?"

"I live in Denver. I'm not quite sure how I got to your cottage, but I don't think it's very far away," Destiny responded, feeling foolish. Why couldn't she remember what happened?

Mrs. Moore smiled. "You might find this strange, but I think I might know what happened. This has happened before."

"What's happened before, Mrs. Moore?"

"Please, call me Clara. Someone suddenly appearing out of nowhere. Of course, the last time it happened was years ago."

Destiny didn't know what to say, so she took a bite of the cookie. It was delicious, and she helped herself to another cookie from the plate.

"What year do you live in?" Clara asked with a gleam in her eyes.

What an odd question. "2017," Destiny answered slowly.

Clara nodded her head and looked delighted at Destiny's answer. "Just as I thought." She took a sip of tea.

"What are you talking about?"

"You have time traveled from where you live in 2017 to my time."

"What?" Destiny asked in shock. "Something strange did happen, but I don't think I time traveled. Time travel isn't real."

"That's what most people think, but it is very real. It just doesn't happen very often."

Destiny set her cookie down, having suddenly lost her appetite. She wondered if Clara was mentally sound.

"So what is the year you live in?" she asked, testing Clara.

"1879. You traveled to my cottage here near Ancroft, England."

"That's impossible!" Destiny almost shouted.

Panic started to well up deep inside her. Her heart was racing so fast, making her head pound in time with her heartbeat.

"Tell me what you were doing just before you found yourself in my gardens," Clara invited calmly, not at all upset at Destiny's words.

Destiny squeezed her eyes shut, hoping that what she was experiencing was just a dream. Instead she pictured herself standing by the painting. She saw herself reaching out to touch the cottage. She remembered the dizziness and vibrations. Was it possible Clara was right? No. It did seem that the elderly woman lived alone. Maybe she was just desperate for company and decided to make up a story to keep Destiny around for awhile.

"If I really did time travel, like you said, why aren't you surprised?"

"Let's just say that I'm familiar with the concept," Clara said after a long hesitation.

They both finished their tea in silence, each keeping their thoughts to themselves. Destiny couldn't wrap her head around the belief that she had actually time traveled, but she decided to not ask any more questions, hoping that she would figure out what was really going on soon enough. She finished the cookies on her plate, but left the tea, since she really wasn't all that fond of that particular type of beverage.

When Clara finally finished her tea, she stood and commented gently. "I know that this is hard for you to believe. I can prove that you are no longer in 2017. I am glad to hear the world has continued that long, by the way."

Destiny didn't say anything. She stayed in her seat while Clara left the kitchen. In a few minutes she was back, carrying what looked like a small bundle of newspapers. "Here is the latest newspaper. I received it a week ago. Our village is small, so we only get a newspaper once a month; not like what is available in the larger cities."

Clara held out the paper and Destiny slowly took it. Forcing herself to look, she saw typed at the top *June 15, 1879*. Destiny let the paper fall to the kitchen table in disbelief.

"I also have a calendar," Clara said, offering a small square paper.

On it, all the months and days were listed, with a cute drawn picture of a kitten on the bottom. On the top was the year 1879 in fancy calligraphy.

"Oh, man," Destiny muttered to herself.

She knew there was one way she could find out for herself if Clara was telling the truth or not. For the first time in a long time, she allowed herself to *feel*. Clara's presence was all over the newspaper and calendar. It was obvious Clara had read each page carefully, enjoying its contents. The calendar also was used. Certain dates were circled in what looked like red paint as if making it known they were important. Deep down she knew Clara was telling the truth and terror coursed through her. If she really did time travel to 1879, to a small village in England of all places, how was she going to get back to her own time?

Chapter Five

*J*une, 2017

"Well, I obviously found the painting," Graham muttered to himself.

He couldn't believe that Destiny had just disappeared right before his eyes. He walked to the doorway of the small room and noted that the gallery was empty. Destiny's boss didn't have any idea that she was no longer there. He turned back to the painting.

Very carefully, he removed the painting from the wall and set it on the floor, leaning it up against the wall. He pulled up his shirt sleeve to uncover his Ziran Watch and quickly put the information in it to return to his time. After that was done, he reached out to touch the painting with his hand that had the watch on it and began to cover the watch with his other hand, but then he hesitated.

He knew he couldn't leave Destiny to wherever she had disappeared. His mind went over the training he had received two years ago when Jack had first offered him the job to be a time-travel agent. One rule was stressed and that was they were to never use the device they were after for any reason. Their job was to find the device, retrieve it, and bring it back to 2045. Even though his training had been drummed into his skull until he could do his job without thinking, he didn't feel good about leaving Destiny in a time period she wasn't familiar with. Graham knew that she most likely had traveled to the time period when the painting was created, the late 1800s. She would not have any idea how to return to her own time. There would be no one to help her. No one except him. He knew he should travel to wherever she had gone and bring her back.

What if she had gotten hurt while she had time traveled or was in danger? He couldn't leave her there. Not when he could help her.

He knew he should contact headquarters through his watch and inform Jack what had just happened, but his gut feeling was telling him that he needed to go after Destiny, immediately. Making his own executive decision, he deleted the information he had just input on his watch. He reached down and picked up the painting, hanging it back on the wall. He made sure his backpack was secure on his back. He glanced around to make sure no one was around to see what he was going to do. Then he took the last step. He touched the painting on the cottage, the exact place Destiny had touched. And he was gone.

Destiny enjoyed spending the rest of the day with Clara, despite the fact that she had traveled, what was it, one hundred and thirty-eight years into the past? When she allowed herself to relax and not think about the fact that she had traveled through time to a small village in 1879 England, she had fun getting to know her new surroundings. Clara immediately started to treat her like a daughter. For some reason, Destiny felt a bond with the older woman that she didn't understand. Clara took her to the nearby ocean to enjoy the spray of water on her face. They spent part of the afternoon in Clara's gardens. Destiny understood that Clara spent quite a bit of her time with her flowers. Clara was very willing to answer all of Destiny's questions, all of them except one. When Destiny asked her about her family, Clara changed the subject. After this had happened for the third time, Destiny got the message. Clara wasn't going to talk about her family.

When the sun started to set, Clara invited her to stay the night. Since Destiny didn't have anywhere else to go, she accepted. Throughout the day, even though she didn't talk to Clara about it, she was thinking about a way she could get back to her time. Since time travel was actually real (since she did travel with the aid of the painting), she should be able to get back to 2017, shouldn't she? She didn't want to even think of the possibility that she might be stuck in 1879 for the rest of her life.

It made sense to her that she needed to find the painting. The *Clara Moore* who created the painting that hung in the gallery and the *Clara Moore* whose cottage she traveled to were most likely the same person. She just needed to find it. From what she could tell, that particular painting didn't hang on any of the walls in the cottage. In fact, Destiny hadn't seen any signs that Clara even painted. But it had to be around somewhere.

"You can sleep in the spare room," Clara told her, as she led Destiny up the stairs. "I hope you will be comfortable here."

"I'm sure I will be," Destiny responded, as they walked up the stairs. Clara had many small paintings on the walls of the hallway, but none of them was the painting.

When Clara paused before a closed door, she placed a hand on Destiny's arm. Destiny wasn't prepared for the contact, so she wasn't able to block the feelings she immediately read from Clara. The older woman was concerned for her and was also feeling a little guilty, along with fondness.

"We will figure out what we can do to help you get back to your time tomorrow," Clara told her sincerely.

"Thank you," Destiny said.

"Sleep well, my dear," Clara said as she opened the door.

Destiny stepped inside and quickly took in the simple room. The floors were well-worn wood covered with braided rugs. There was a small bed covered with a quilt against one wall and a large wardrobe against another. She immediately loved it.

There was a nightgown that Clara had obviously laid out on the bed. For a split second, Destiny debated as to whether she should change into it or not and

decided to go ahead. She hated sleeping in her jeans. After changing, she slipped into the bed and found it surprisingly comfortable.

For the next few hours she tossed and turned. Now that she had time to think, all she could think about was that she was in a bed in a cottage in 1879 England. She still couldn't believe that she'd actually traveled through time. She went through the steps over and over again in her mind, trying to figure out how it had exactly happened. The idea of being stuck in this time started to scare her to death.

She'd never believed in time travel. Although many books and movies had been made about the subject, it wasn't a top interest to her. In the few books she had actually read, the person who had traveled through time never could return to their own time, or if they could, the window to actually return was not always able to be used. Tears ran down her face at the thought of never seeing her time again.

She quickly dried her face with the sleeve of her nightgown and decided that she needed to do something rather than lie in bed and wonder what would happen next. It made sense to her that if she touched the painting in her time which brought her to the exact place which was depicted, the painting was somewhere in Clara's cottage.

Finally deciding that she couldn't sleep, she got up. While Clara was sleeping, she would explore the cottage and look for the painting. Clara had left a lit lantern in her room, and Destiny hadn't wanted to blow out the flame, preferring not to be in the darkness in a place she wasn't familiar with. Picking up the lantern she carried it to the door, opened it, and quietly tiptoed down the hall. There were two other rooms on the second floor, and both doors were closed. Which one was Clara's? Following her feelings, she quietly opened one of them. She peered inside and gasped, instantly knowing she had found what she was looking for.

The room was small, but it was very obvious that it was used for painting. There were half-finished canvases all over the room. Destiny held the lantern in front of her, and quickly examined the paintings. There were at least ten of them in various stages of completion. There was one on an easel half finished. None of them was the painting she was looking for, and she sighed with disappointment. As she turned to leave, she saw another stack of canvases that she hadn't looked through in a corner of the room. She set the lantern down on the floor and carefully looked through each one. And there it was, the very last one. But it wasn't finished. Just like the others in the room, it was only half done. Why didn't Clara finish any of them? Destiny pulled the painting away from the stack and leaned it against the wall. Holding the lantern up, she could see that the cottage had only been roughly drawn in. The sky had been finished, along with the stone path that led to the sea. She reached out and touched the drawn-in cottage, hoping it would take her back to 2017, but of course it didn't. Obviously, the painting needed to be finished for it to work. But what had made it a time-traveling device in the first place?

Clara was so disappointed that tears started to form in her eyes. From the little she understood about time travel, she knew she wouldn't be able to return to her time, and the entire situation terrified her. Somehow she was going to need to convince Clara to finish this painting, and as quickly as possible. Picking up the lantern, she left the room and practically ran down the stairs and out into the night, not remembering that she was still in the nightgown.

The moon was full, so Destiny could find her way in the dark quite easily. She blew the lantern out and set it down near the door. She ran barefoot down the stone path and towards the ocean. She didn't stop until she was at the edge of the water. Letting the water lap against her ankles, she stood looking into the darkness, trying to let the sound of the waves calm her. Suddenly she saw a movement in the corner of her eye.

She turned to see who it was and was shocked when she saw Graham walking towards her. Was this day going to get any crazier?

"Oh, good, I found you," Graham said with a grin, not seeming the least bit surprised that she was standing in front of him.

"You found me?" Destiny asked with relief, suddenly desperately wanting to hug him. "Do you mean you know what happened?"

"Well, it was kind of obvious. You touched an old painting and disappeared."

Destiny frowned at him. "You knew this could happen, didn't you? That's why you were so interested in the painting. You should have told me."

"Oh, really? And if I had said to you, Destiny, I want to buy that painting, because if someone touches it they are going to be transported back in time, would you have believed me?"

Destiny had nothing to say to that. She wouldn't have believed him. Why should she have? Until she actually did time travel, she had only believed that it was fiction.

"How long have you been here?" she asked instead.

"Since the sun was setting. I wanted to look around. When it became dark, I decided it would be best to wait until morning to announce my presence."

Destiny couldn't help herself. She was so glad to see Graham that she threw herself into his arms. His strong arms caught her in surprise, but then he pulled her close and held her for a moment.

Destiny loved being in his arms. She had only met him the day before, and that was briefly, but for some reason she suddenly felt she had known him forever. She was very grateful he knew what had happened when she had touched the painting and had somehow known he needed to go after her. After a few moments in his arms, she pulled away, embarrassed at how she had acted. Here she was, in 1879, standing in front of the most handsome man she'd ever seen, in a nightgown of all things. Of course, the nightgown was much more modest than some dresses women wore in her time. It was made of thick flannel and covered her from head to toe, but it was principle of the thing, wasn't it?

When she stepped back, she opened her mouth to ask him a question, but stopped at the look in his eyes. They looked like a dark blue in the moonlit night, and she knew that, if she allowed him to touch her again, she would be flooded with his feelings. She stepped back even further, not sure if she wanted to know what he was thinking or feeling.

Graham started to pace. "I came to take you back home."

Destiny's face lit up in the moonlight. "You can take me home? Back to 2017? Well, let's go."

He started to respond but instead looked behind her, and Destiny whirled around to see what captured his attention. Clara was making her way toward them.

"So, we have another traveler, do we?" were Clara's first words to Graham.

"Hello, ma'am," Graham responded, as he stepped next to Destiny and put his arm around her.

The older woman looked back and forth between the two of them, a knowing and pleased look in her eyes. "You must know each other."

Destiny spoke up. "Actually, we just met yesterday." Immediately she felt a closeness to Graham that she had not felt for any other man, and she blocked the feelings.

"Let's go back to my cottage," Clara invited them. "It is very late. It seems we need to talk, but I do think it can wait until morning."

Destiny opened her mouth to argue. She was aware that if Graham knew how to follow her, he very likely would know how to get back, and she wanted to get back to her time as soon as possible. But Graham spoke over her.

"That would be fine, ma'am."

Destiny turned to glare at Graham, but he kept his arm around her and squeezed her shoulders, as if urging her to not say anything. She took a deep breath and kept her mouth shut. It was obvious that he had another purpose for being here besides to collect her. And she subconsciously knew that, if they returned to 2017 now, she wouldn't get her many questions answered.

She followed Clara, with Graham behind her, back to the cottage. Once they entered the small home, Clara told Graham he could spend the night on her couch. Destiny found it humorous that Clara didn't go into her room until she knew that Destiny was in her room with the door shut.

For some strange reason, she felt comforted that Graham was nearby. Once this was all over, and she was back safe and sound, she was going to quiz Graham and learn exactly how time travel worked. The fact that he didn't seem concerned that she had disappeared from the gallery, and he had somehow known what to do to follow her, she knew that he was her best bet to learn all she could about the subject. She made a promise to herself that she would learn exactly how time travel worked. Before she knew it, she fell into a deep sleep.

Chapter Six

T he next morning Destiny woke to the smell of coffee and bacon, and her stomach growled in anticipation. She hadn't eaten very much the night before because of the continued thoughts of the fact that she had actually time traveled to England and was in 1879. When she first woke up, she kept her eyes closed, hoping when she opened them, she would be in her own room, but when she finally did look, she saw the homemade quilt, light-blue cotton curtains, and a scarred wooden chair where she had put her clothes. Destiny sat up in her bed and saw that a light-yellow dress with small blue flowers had been placed at the foot of her bed.

She got out of bed and picked up the dress and instantly hated it. She never wore yellow since it washed out her face and made her look pale with her blonde, almost white hair. She assumed that Clara had put the dress on her bed while she was still asleep. She knew Clara was hinting that Destiny needed to dress to fit in with the time period she was now in.

Dropping the dress onto the bed, she sat down and sighed, knowing she had a huge decision to make. Now that Graham was here, she wondered what his plans were. A thought crept into her mind as she glanced at the ugly dress. She could either leave the room in her own clothing and insist that Graham take her back to their time, or she could put the dress on and take advantage of this experience of being in Clara's time period, knowing that Graham could take them both back to 2017 whenever they needed to leave.

She stood and looked out of the small window and saw that it overlooked Clara's gardens. She could see the path that led down to the ocean. Making an instant decision, she turned and slipped off her nightgown. Pulling the dress over her head, she was surprised that it fit her perfectly. After she buttoned up the dress, she looked down and saw stockings and black shoes on the floor. She picked up one of the shoes and frowned. It looked very uncomfortable. Making a quick decision, she slipped on her own brown pumps. She would wear the ugly black shoes if she went anywhere.

Opening the bedroom door, she followed her nose downstairs and into the kitchen. She found Graham standing at the stove frying bacon, and her heart skipped a beat. She recalled how she had practically thrown herself at him the night before and how he had held her in comfort.

"Good morning, my dear," Clara said when she saw Destiny hesitate at the doorway of the kitchen. "The dress fits you perfectly."

Graham turned from the stove and looked at her, his eyes widening. Destiny noticed that he was also dressed according to the time period, and she wondered where he had gotten the clothing. From what she could gather, there weren't any signs that Clara shared the cottage with a man.

"Good morning," Destiny returned Clara's greeting.

"Come in and sit down. Would you like a cup of coffee or tea?"

Destiny stared at Graham for almost a full minute before she realized what she was doing and shook her head as if to clear it. "Coffee, please."

Clara smiled. "I don't enjoy coffee that much. I prefer a good cup of tea, but I do know that Americans like their coffee."

Graham picked up a cup that was sitting on the counter near him and gestured to Clara. "Coffee is a great way to start the day."

Destiny grinned at him as she accepted a cup from Clara. She took a sip and then set it down on the table. "Can I help with anything?"

"You may set the table, if you wish. The dishes are in that cupboard, and the silverware is in that drawer."

Destiny reached into the cupboard and started to set three plates on the table. Clara had placed a lace tablecloth on the table, and Destiny had a hard time covering it up, because it was so pretty. But soon she had three place settings ready to be used.

In no time at all, the food was placed on the table. Besides the bacon and coffee, there were pancakes, scrambled eggs, fried potatoes, and fruit, along with huge muffins. Her eyes widened at the amount of food that had been prepared for the three of them. After Clara said a prayer over the meal, they filled their plates. Destiny tried to only take a little bit, placing a muffin and a small spoonful of eggs on her plate.

"My dear, you need to eat more than that," Clara chastised her, as she added a large spoonful of potatoes to Destiny's plate. "Breakfast is the most important meal of the day."

"Thank you," Destiny said wryly, as she exchanged glances with Graham. She never ate a large breakfast. Usually she only had a bagel with a glass of orange juice, but it looked like she would be eating large breakfasts while she was in 1879, especially if Clara had anything to say about it.

She had to admit that she was hungry and started to dig into the potatoes, but she wished she had ketchup to add. Was ketchup even invented in 1879? Probably not.

"Can I ask you a question?" Destiny asked Clara when all three were almost done with their meal.

"Of course," Clara agreed with a question in her eyes.

"Why weren't you surprised to learn that Graham is also from the future? Most people would be shocked or even scared to find that out."

Clara sighed and sat back in her chair. For a few moments she was silent; then she spoke. "Would you both like to go to market with me this morning?"

Destiny felt confused, and she opened her mouth to ask another question, but she stopped when Graham covered her hand with his under the table. It was obvious he was telling her to let it go.

"That sounds like fun," Destiny said instead, although she wanted to insist that Clara answer her question.

"I'm not sure if we should let ourselves be seen by other people in your time, Clara," Graham broke in, looking at Clara and then at Destiny. "In fact, I think we should get you back to your time as soon as possible."

Clara seemed disappointed in Graham's suggestion, but she smiled serenely in agreement. Destiny didn't say anything, but she privately wondered if it would hurt if they could stay for awhile. Since they were already in the year 1879, why not stay and explore for a bit?

As soon as breakfast was over, Clara started to clear the table. Both Destiny and Graham helped with the dishes. Destiny watched as Clara took a small bar of soap and cut thin slices off of it. After swirling the soap in the hot water, she started to wash the dishes. While Destiny watched Clara efficiently do the daily chore, she was fascinated. She had never really washed dishes by hand like this in her time except for a few pans. She had her dishwasher. She realized that, besides the obvious differences between her time and Clara's, many things had been invented to make jobs and life much easier.

Clara broke into her thoughts. "I'm sure washing dishes is different in your time."

Destiny realized that Clara had noticed her intense interest. "Quite a bit. We have a machine called a dishwasher. I just need to scrape loose food from the dishes and then they are put on two racks. I add soap and turn on the machine. All the dishes are washed and dried in about an hour."

"I'm not sure it's a good idea to talk about the future with Clara," Graham interrupted.

"Why not?" Destiny asked curiously.

"Graham glanced at Clara but before he could answer, the older woman broke into the conversation.

"I'm aware that great progress has been made in the future, probably even more than I can imagine."

"I don't know if it's a good idea that you know what the progress is," Graham argued.

Destiny decided to change the subject. "Graham, I'd really like Clara to show us her village. We are already dressed in her time, although I guess I'll need to have Clara help me with my hair, since I have no idea how to put my hair in those fancy twists."

When Destiny mentioned her hair, she noticed that Graham instantly focused on it. The thoughts that were running through his mind were so strong, it was if Destiny could read his mind. She instantly knew he wanted to run his fingers through her hair and was doing everything he could to keep himself from doing so. She touched it herself, knowing Graham was seeing long wavy blonde hair that hung just past her shoulders, with a few dark highlights that her hairdresser had added just the week before.

"Graham?" Destiny questioned. "Are you alright?" She smiled to herself, because she knew his thoughts, and she flicked her hair with her hand, deciding it wouldn't hurt to flirt a bit.

Graham shook his head slightly as if to clear his thoughts. He needed to forget his attraction to Destiny and focus on the job he came to do. He wanted to insist that they return to their time as soon as breakfast was over, but he admitted to himself that he was also curious about what life was like in 1879. It was a time period he hadn't had the opportunity to visit yet. And besides, he still needed to figure out how Clara's paintings had become time-travel devices. If he could figure out that puzzle, it would be easier to collect her other paintings and bring them to his time.

He slowly nodded his head in agreement. "Okay. If I agree to stay, will you agree that we go back to your time when I say we need to go?"

"Of course," Destiny agreed. Her smoky-gray eyes lit up with delight, and Graham was glad he had agreed.

Clara also looked pleased that she was going to have company for another day. "You both should probably pretend that you are married."

"To each other?" Destiny squeaked.

"Well, of course," Clara said, puzzled. "It is going to be hard to explain to some of my neighbors who you are, and it will be easier if I can introduce you as a couple."

Graham grinned, a twinkle in his eyes. "Sounds like a good idea to me."

Destiny shook her head. "I don't think we need to pretend we're married. After today, anyone who meets us will never see us again."

Clara thought for a moment and then looked at Graham. "We can say that you are my nephew visiting from London. It's far enough away that no one will suspect anything." She turned to Destiny. "I'm sorry, dear. But you really need to pretend to be married. Maybe things are more relaxed in your time, but in mine, it is considered scandalous for a woman to travel with a man alone, without a chaperone. Well-bred ladies never go anywhere without a female companion unless they are married. If you want to fit in and you don't want uncomfortable questions, you will need to pretend to be married."

Destiny reluctantly agreed, nodding her head. What would it hurt? After all, she wouldn't be here, in this time, for very long. No one that they would meet would likely even remember that they were there. Clara put the last dish away in a cupboard and touched Destiny's shoulder.

"Come, let's do your hair, and then we can leave." She looked at Graham. "I do have a carriage we can use, but I often walk to the village if it's nice weather. Since it's such a nice day, do you mind if we walk? It will take about an hour to get there."

"We can walk. Let's keep to whatever schedule you normally have. I know we will be meeting people, but I want to stand out as little as possible."

Destiny followed Clara out of the room and up the stairs. Graham stayed seated. He closed his eyes and leaned back in his chair. He knew he gave in to the trip to town to see Destiny's face light up with her beautiful smile. If his boss knew what they were going to be doing that morning, he would not be happy. He sighed and stood to his feet and headed outside. There was a fine mist that came from the nearby ocean which that covered the ground, but it was lifting, and he could see Clara's well-kept flower gardens. He decided he would take a short walk while the two women readied themselves for the day.

Chapter Seven

Destiny sat in a cushioned chair in front of a dressing table, watching intently while Clara worked some magic and prepared her hair. She started to brush it out with a fancy hairbrush. Her hair hung a few inches below her shoulders, but Destiny liked to have it loose and free. She usually developed headaches when she pulled her hair back with elastics or clips. If she had her way, she would wear it down, but she knew women in Clara's time always wore their hair up, and she needed to do the same. Even if she developed a headache from the weird-looking pins Clara was sticking into her hair, it would be worth it to experience more of 1879. Considering how upset and scared she was the night before and the excitement she felt now, she was determined to experience all that she could, for she knew her little adventure would soon end. She would be back in 2017 working in the gallery and living her uneventful life soon enough.

Clara broke into her musings. "I'm curious. Why are you so reluctant to pretend you are married to Graham for a few hours?"

Destiny was startled at Clara's question, and she didn't say anything.

"We can come up with another story as to why you are both here, if you are really uncomfortable with the idea," Clara offered, as she slipped another pin into Destiny's hair.

"It's okay. I was just surprised, I guess. I have only known Graham for a few days."

"I wonder if there is more to it than that."

"What do you mean?" Destiny asked, not sure she wanted to know what Clara was thinking.

"I haven't always been alone. I know what it's like to meet a man and instantly have that connection with him, like you are soulmates and meeting each other was meant to be."

"Have you been married then?" Destiny asked curiously, but also to get the conversation off of herself.

"Yes, for only a few months," Clara responded with sadness in her voice.

"What happened?"

"He...went on a business trip, and I never saw him again."

Destiny wanted to ask more questions, but it was obvious by the sadness in Clara's voice that she didn't want to talk about it. "I'm sorry."

Clara shrugged her thin shoulders. "It was a long, long time ago." She put the last pin into Destiny's hair. "There. Now you look like you were born in this time."

Even though there was a mirror on the dressing table, Destiny had stopped watching what Clara had been doing. When she looked in the mirror, she smiled. Clara had twisted and then secured her hair to the back of her head. A few strands of hair framed her face. She had to admit Clara had done a great job.

"Let's find Graham and let him know we are ready to go," Clara said as she handed Destiny a wrap.

They both left Clara's room. As Destiny passed the room where she had seen the paintings, she almost stopped to ask Clara about them. The older woman continued down the stairs, talking about some of the things they might see, and Destiny decided her questions could wait until they returned.

They found Graham sitting on a bench near the flower gardens, his face towards the sea. He stood when he heard them coming. "Your sea is beautiful."

Clara looked pleased at Graham's words. "I've been blessed to live here all my life."

"So you grew up here?" Destiny asked, as the three of them started walking in the direction of the village. It was a cool morning, and she was grateful for the wrap Clara had given her. She pulled it more tightly around her.

"Yes. I was born in the room you are using. I have a brother and a sister."

"Where do they live?"

"My brother moved to London as soon as he was grown. He always hated living in a small village such as ours. My sister... passed on a few years back."

So Clara was truly all alone, Destiny thought to herself.

"When my sister married, she moved into her husband's home. It was a second marriage for him, and he was already established. My mother died when I was eighteen, and my father died a few years later. Even though I am the youngest of my siblings, since neither of them wanted the cottage, I inherited it."

Destiny thought how sad it was that Clara had lost so many of her family, but she knew it wasn't uncommon to have family members die so early in this time period. She thought of her own family. She didn't have any siblings. It had only been herself and her parents. They were both doctors. Her father was a cardiac surgeon, and her mother was a pediatrician. Destiny had pretty much raised herself. They never really understood their only daughter. Once she was grown and on her own, Destiny had little contact with them beyond the occasional dinner during the holidays. She knew they were disappointed that she hadn't followed in their footsteps to become a doctor and instead had studied art and now worked in an art gallery in Denver.

While they walked, it started to warm up. The mist from the ocean disappeared, and soon Destiny was able to remove her wrap. When she undid the large button at the nape of her neck, she felt strong hands slip the wrap from her shoulders. She smiled her thanks at Graham, and he draped it over his arm. Her hand brushed against his arm, and a tingle ran through her body. She moved away slightly, but she had the sudden strong desire to hold his hand. What where these feelings? Was Clara right when she said that sometimes you meet someone, and there is an instant connection?

She shook her head to clear her thoughts and forced herself to look at her surroundings. What she saw was typical of where she'd imagined English villages to be located, with rolling green hills. Small cottages dotted the landscape periodically, some with hedges surrounding them, used as fences. She saw the occasional cattle and horses, and she could hear a dog barking in the distance. Destiny saw a woman hanging clothes on a rope outside of one cottage. Clara called out a greeting as they passed but didn't stop.

When they finally entered the village, Destiny immediately fell in love with it. The main street was lined with small cottages. Then as they approached the heart of the village, there were quaint shops and small wagons along the cobble street.

She watched silently as Clara picked out a few fresh fruits and vegetables from a wagon, talking to the owners. Destiny noticed that Clara didn't rush through her shopping. She took her time, inspecting the produce carefully. While she made her selections, she talked to the owners, asking questions about their families. Destiny listened, and she learned that one woman's daughter had had a baby just the day before. Another man accepted Clara's condolences, as he talked about his sick wife. At one time, a few children approached Clara, and she stooped down to their level and asked about their schooling. Destiny could tell that Clara cared deeply about the people in her village.

Again, she couldn't help but compare the time she was now in with her own. In Clara's time, no one seemed in a hurry. They enjoyed each other's company and were willing to spend the time needed to get caught up on the events in their lives. After Clara purchased her fresh produce, she led Destiny and Graham into a type of general store. The woman who owned this store looked up as they entered, a small bell rang that announced their arrival.

She smiled with delight at seeing Clara. "I'm so glad you came this morning," she said, as she greeted her with a hug.

"Hi, Doris," Clara said, as she returned the hug, but Destiny could tell she was reluctant. "Let me introduce my guests."

She quickly told Doris their names, like she had done with the other people they had met. When Clara had introduced Destiny and Graham to the previous people, they were greeted politely back. Clara had been able to keep them from asking too many personal questions, but she wasn't able to with Doris.

"Where did you say you were from?" Doris asked, interest in her eyes.

"We are friends of Clara's nephew who lives in London," Graham broke in easily, changing their initial story slightly. "We were just married and are taking a holiday to this part of England before settling into our new lives together."

Destiny squirmed a bit at the made-up story, but she knew it couldn't be helped. She suddenly realized part of her wished it was true, that they were married, and this thought made her squirm even more.

"How interesting," Doris said, as she looked at Clara carefully.

"We can't stay long," Clara said, as she gave the other woman a small list of things she needed to purchase. "Can you fill this for me?"

Destiny could tell that Doris wanted to ask more questions, but she eventually turned away and started to gather up the things Clara had on the list. Clara took Destiny's arm and pulled her towards the back of the store. Graham followed them both.

"We need to be careful what we say to Doris," Clara whispered to them. "She is the village's biggest gossip."

Destiny and Graham nodded their understanding. Graham then took Destiny's hand and slid it through the crook of his arm. "Let's look at those books on that shelf."

Clara looked relieved, as they walked away towards the books. There was *The Bible, Heidi, The Adventures of Huckleberry Finn, Wuthering Heights,* among others. They all looked like they had leather covers. Then she saw *Pride and Prejudice* and gasped, as she took it off the shelf and opened the cover almost reverently.

"Look at this," Destiny breathed. "I love this book." She opened it and saw from the copyright information that it was a first edition copy.

Clara was standing behind them and heard Destiny's words. "This book is still around in your time?" she questioned softly, after glancing at Doris to make sure she was far enough away to not hear her words.

Destiny nodded. "It's one of my favorites."

"Then let me buy this for you."

"Oh, I couldn't let you do that." Destiny protested, glancing at Graham to see his reaction. He seemed content to let her decide.

"Please let me," Clara pleaded.

Destiny hesitated but then nodded, as she could tell that purchasing the book would mean a lot to Clara. "Okay." She had seen that the book only cost a few pennies, but she hoped it wasn't too much for Clara.

Destiny knew that this gift would be something she would never be able to show anyone in her time, but it would also be something she would always treasure, a souvenir of her time-travel experience.

As Clara purchased the items she needed, Doris kept up a running conversation of questions, mostly directed towards Graham and Destiny. They answered them in the shortest way possible. Destiny breathed a sigh of relief when they finally were able to leave the store.

"I probably shouldn't have taken you into Doris's store," Clara commented as they walked down the street. "But she would have heard that I had guests, and I would have had a visit from her this afternoon. I decided it would be better to just get it over with."

"It's fine," Graham said. "We can't expect people to not have questions, but I do think it would be a good idea if we left now."

Clara nodded in agreement. "I wanted to take you to a small restaurant for tea, but we can eat some of the fruit I purchased instead."

In almost no time, the small village was behind them. For a few minutes, Destiny listened silently while Clara and Graham talked to each other. When there was a break in their conversation, Destiny touched Clara's arm and asked the question that had been on her mind since she had arrived the day before. She had already tried to ask Clara her questions twice, but the older woman had refused to answer. She decided to try again.

"Clara, I am curious about something. When I arrived yesterday, you seemed to know immediately that I was from the future. How did you know that?"

Clara hesitated, and Destiny was sure that she was going to just ignore her question, but then she started talking.

"Years ago, only a few months after my father's death, I was living in my cottage alone. My brother and sister had married and were gone. I was very lonely. I spent quite a bit of time walking along the ocean's shore. One day on one of my walks, I met a man I had never seen before. Back then, it was rare for this area to have any visitors. He said his name was Marcus, and he was looking for family members. But that didn't make sense. After all, I've lived here all my life, and I had never heard of the people he was looking for.

"He also acted very strange. He seemed amazed at my small cottage. He was dressed very differently. He had on black pants, a white shirt, and green velvet vest, with weird looking, black shoes. He was a happy man, always smiling with rosy cheeks, and he had the greenest eyes I'd ever seen. I immediately fell for him."

"He is the man you were telling me about," Destiny broke in. "The man you said was your soulmate."

Clara's eyes pierced her own. "Yes. To make a long story short, we fell in love and were married only a few weeks later. We lived in my cottage and were very happy together. There were strange things about him, though. Like he didn't know how to run a wood stove or even boil water on it. When we went to the village, he seemed amazed at his surroundings, as if he was seeing certain things for the first time. He refused to talk about his family or where he was from. After we were married for a few months, I finally demanded that he tell me where he was from, where he grew up, and where his family was. I knew he was keeping some very large secrets, and that isn't good for a marriage.

"One night he told me he was from the future, from 1943. His family had immigrated to America, and there was a war going on that he didn't want to be part of. He had found an old golden key that turned out to be a time-travel device. Even though he refused to show me how it worked, he did let me see and hold the key only one time. It was about three inches long and looked like pure gold, although parts of it were tarnished. It was obvious it was very old. The most interesting part of the key was that it vibrated when I held it. Marcus told me I was feeling the power of the key. After Marcus showed me the key, he hid it somewhere, and I never saw it again."

Graham chuckled. "He sounds like my boss. He owns a velvet green vest with black pants. He says he likes to look like a leprechaun."

Clara smiled. "I teased him about his clothing. Once we married, he put them away in a trunk, and I never saw him wear them again. After we were married six months, I had the best, but also the worst, day of my life. I discovered I was pregnant. I had suspected for a few weeks, but I was able to confirm it with the village doctor."

Clara stopped walking, and her eyes looked off into the distance, as if remembering that specific day. "I didn't want to tell Marcus about the doctor's appointment. I didn't want to make a big deal about it if I was wrong. I ended up spending most of that day in the village. I had some shopping to do, and I visited with a close friend. When I finally returned, Marcus wasn't at home. At first I wasn't alarmed. Every once in awhile he would disappear and be gone all day. He would always be home for dinner though, so I was never concerned about his ramblings. When I asked him where he went, he would tell me that he liked to explore.

"But that day, he never returned. I remember looking all over for him. I spent days going around to the villages nearby. No one had seen him. He had just...disappeared. I never saw him again."

"What do you think happened to him?" Graham asked, looking at Clara intently.

Clara started to walk again. "It took me awhile, but I finally came to the conclusion that he had used the golden key to time travel somewhere. And for whatever reason, he wasn't able to return. I even started to wonder if that was what he was doing when he would sometimes disappear for the entire day, using the key to time travel."

Clara had tears in her eyes, as she finished her story, and Destiny put an arm around her in comfort. It was obvious that even though Marcus had disappeared over twenty years ago, she still grieved for him.

"What happened to your baby?" Destiny asked, after they walked in silence for a few minutes.

"I had a baby girl," Clara confessed. "After she was born, I made a horrible mistake. My older sister wasn't able to have children. She had been in a carriage accident, and the result was that she wasn't able to conceive. In my grief, my sister and her husband convinced me that it would be better if they raised my baby. It would be better if my daughter be raised in a stable home with a mother and a father. They also didn't believe that I had been actually legally married to Marcus. We married secretly and quickly. We had gone on a trip to Scotland and was married there. No one we knew witnessed the marriage besides the priest who married us. After Marcus disappeared, rumors had started that Marcus had been a drifter who had taken advantage of me, resulting in a bastard baby. For my baby's sake, I was convinced I needed to give her up. So I did."

Destiny sighed with sadness. She felt so sorry for Clara and all she had gone through. Up until that moment, she had thought of her time-travel experience as a horrible mistake, and then, after Graham had showed up, a fun adventure. She hadn't thought of it being something that could turn out so badly. She understood a bit more why Graham was so worried about how time travel could change history.

Clara tried to smile brightly through her tears. "It is nice to talk to someone about this. No one knows my story. Because of the time-travel aspect of the entire story, I can't talk to anyone about what happened."

"Do you ever see your daughter? What is her name?" Destiny asked.

"My sister did allow me to name her. I gave her the name of Katherine Mary. But no, I have no contact with her. After she was born, my sister and her husband moved away. I have no idea where she is. I never heard from them again."

Destiny felt anger at Clara's sister. She couldn't imagine how awful that would have been to have a child taken from her and to never see her again.

"I know I can't undo my past, but I wish now that I had kept her and refused to allow my sister to convince me into giving her up. I have a trust fund that is connected to this cottage that I live on. I could have sold the cottage and moved somewhere else. I didn't have to stay here. But I was so lost in my grief because of Marcus's disappearance, that I couldn't see any other options until months after Katherine was born."

Throughout the entire conversation, Graham had said little. Destiny had glanced at him from time to time while Clara talked, and she noticed that her story was upsetting to him, what had happened to her. She thought about Graham's comment that Clara's description of Marcus sounded a lot like his boss. Was there a connection there? Did Graham know more that he was willing to share?

Clara wiped her eyes and smiled at them both, and Destiny knew the conversation was over. She could see the cottage in the distance, and she felt disappointment. For some reason, she didn't want the walk to end.

"So, now that we all know about time travel, what year are you from?"

Graham didn't say anything, so Destiny decided to answer for both of them, wondering if Clara had forgotten that she had already told her. "We are from 2017."

Clara shook her head in amazement. "I know that you are from 2017, dear. I am wondering what year Graham is from."

Graham cleared his throat. "I'm actually from 2045."

Destiny looked at Graham in shock. "What do you mean?"

He didn't say anything, just looked at her intently, as if trying to tell her something.

"That's very interesting," Clara commented, missing the exchange between Destiny and Graham. "It's so hard to imagine life continuing on for so many years. But life does go on, for all of us, no matter where we live on this earth. So between the three of us, we represent three different time periods. It would be so much fun to hear about what life is like in 2017 and 2045."

Graham shook his head fiercely. "I don't think that is a wise idea."

Clara shrugged her shoulders. "Most likely not."

Destiny was still in shock that Graham was not from 2017. "Why didn't you tell me that you are also from the future?" she asked Graham. For some reason that she couldn't explain, she was very hurt that he hadn't confided in her that specific fact.

"It's not something that I wanted to convey at that time."

Something in Graham's voice warned her that he wasn't going to answer anymore of her questions, and the three of them walked the rest of the short distance to the Clara's cottage in silence. Once they arrived in front of the cottage, Destiny suddenly couldn't stand being around him anymore. Why did he keep the year he was from a secret? What else was he hiding from her? She excused herself quietly, turned around, and ran down the narrow path towards the beach.

Chapter Eight

Graham sighed, as he ran his fingers through his hair. "I guess I shouldn't have told her that I'm not from her time."

He knew that Destiny would be upset when she found out he wasn't from her time. He had hoped he could have kept that information from her indefinitely, but there was also a part of him that wanted her to know the truth, and he was glad Clara had pushed the issue.

Clara smiled. "No, I think it was right you did tell her. She is upset for another reason."

Graham looked at Clara when she didn't continue her thoughts. "Care to clue me in why you think she is upset?"

"I think it would be best if you follow her and ask her yourself."

Graham hesitated and then nodded. "I'll help you carry these packages inside, and then I will go find her."

After going inside and placing the packages on the kitchen table, Clara placed a hand on his arm, stopping him as he turned to leave.

"Please promise me one thing."

"Okay," Graham agreed.

"Promise me that you do not time travel back to your time or Destiny's without saying goodbye."

"I promise," Graham said with a smile.

Graham sighed as he left the cottage. If his boss knew that he had told Destiny what year he was from, he most likely would be fired, or the very least demoted from being a *Time-Travel Guardian*. But for some reason that he couldn't explain, he had a strong feeling that she needed to know, and he could only hope that his boss would eventually understand.

He took his time walking down to the ocean so he could gather his thoughts. The stone path was smooth under his feet until it ended abruptly at the edge of Clara's property, fading into the sandy beach. He could see Destiny in the distance. She was sitting among a large group of ragged rocks. As he walked closer, he could tell that these rocks were likely buried under the water twice a day because of the tides, but for now they were dry, although the spray of the ocean occasionally hit some of them.

Destiny didn't look up as he joined her on a nearby rock. For a long time, they both sat in silence, as they watched the ocean and the wildlife around them.

"I love the ocean," Destiny said, breaking the silence. "I used to live in California near the beach. Even though I now live in Denver, when I get a chance, I take my vacations along the coast somewhere. The water is so soothing to me, but sometimes it seems it can change in an instant when a storm comes."

Graham didn't reply, content to allow her to talk.

"I guess you might be expecting an apology for getting angry. I don't know why it upsets me that you aren't from 2017. Even though we both time traveled to Clara's time, I guess it never occurred to me that time travel could happen in my future, 2045. I feel stupid to not have realized that."

"I am from 2045. I work for a secret government agency and am called a *Time-Travel Guardian*. I am sent all over the world and to all different time periods to collect time-travel devices. I try to do this without anyone around me knowing that I'm not from their time. Once I find the time-travel device I'm after, I return it to my time, and it is kept in a large warehouse for safekeeping."

Destiny's mouth dropped open in amazement. "Seriously? You mean there are more time-travel devices besides the painting in Aurora's art gallery and the golden key Clara told us about?"

"There are time-travel devices all over the place. It is the agent's job to figure out what they are, where they are, and how they work."

"Why do you have to collect them all?"

"Because time-travel devices are dangerous. They change history. They change people's lives. I mean, look at what happened with Clara and Marcus. He somehow found a golden key and used it to travel to Clara's time. He met her. They got married. Most likely he was using that key to travel to other places after they married, for whatever reason. What he should have done was to have buried the key or to somehow have gotten rid of it. He didn't. He kept using it."

"What do you think happened to Marcus?"

"He probably did use the key to travel somewhere else when Clara had gone to the village that day. Something happened. Maybe the key stopped working. Maybe something happened in the time period he traveled to that stopped him from coming back to Clara. We will probably never know. But because of his choices, Clara became pregnant. She felt she had to give up her daughter. In my opinion, Marcus changed Clara's history, along with their daughter's."

Destiny nodded her head in understanding. "If Marcus hadn't used the key to begin with, Clara probably would have met and fallen in love with someone else. She wouldn't have spent her life all alone. She would have had children who could be with her as she grows old."

"Do you see how dangerous time travel is? In my time, we have discovered that as people find these devices, whether they are used out of curiosity or for ill intentions, they are still changing history. So *Time-Travel Guardians* were formed."

"Are there really that many time-travel devices in the world that an actual agency had to be formed?"

"You wouldn't believe me if I told you how many there are."

"In 2017, time travel is considered fiction. I haven't heard of anyone who has actually found one. There are many books about it and movies. But they are fiction."

"Or are they?" Graham asked with a slight smile.

"What do you mean?"

"What if these books or movies are true stories, the experiences of the person who wrote them. They just made them into fiction because no one would believe them anyway."

Destiny didn't say anything for a few minutes, as she thought about what Graham said. "I guess that could be what's happening. It's hard to believe though."

"It's hard to believe anything that doesn't have a logical explanation," Graham said. "There isn't a logical explanation of how most time-travel devices work, why they work the way they do, or what makes them into time-travel devices."

"I have to admit that if I hadn't experienced it myself, I wouldn't believe it."

"Precisely my point."

"So, do people in 2045 believe that time travel is no longer fiction?"

"Yes, most people have accepted that time travel is real, which is another reason why it is so dangerous. There are many out there who are searching for these devices on their own, to be used for their own gain, not to just experience an adventure. That is another one of my jobs, to stop these devices from falling into the wrong hands."

"That's very interesting. 2045 is less than thirty years ahead of 2017. In the grand scheme of things, that isn't very a long period of time. What made people start believing in time travel?"

Graham hesitated. "I can't tell you that. To tell you would change *your* history."

Destiny looked frustrated, like she was going to argue with him, demanding that he tell her, but she didn't, knowing that her efforts would be useless.

"Do you think Clara knows that her painting is a time-travel device?"

Graham shook his head. "I don't think she has any idea. Actually only some of her paintings are devices. But I know my boss is trying to collect all of them since we don't know which ones are time travel devices and which ones aren't."

"I know where the painting is right now."

"What do you mean?"

"I confess that I snooped a little last night, before you showed up. There is a room next to mine that she uses as a painting room. There are many paintings in there. It's like she paints something, but then doesn't do anything with it."

"Yes, I know what you mean. I looked around her cottage while she was fixing your hair this morning. I didn't see even one of her paintings on her walls."

"Well, I did see the painting that took me here, but it isn't finished yet. In fact, quite a few of her paintings aren't finished."

"That's interesting."

"Aurora told me Clara's history once. She created many paintings in her lifetime, but she only gave away a few of them. Most of them were stored in her house, and no one saw them. It was only after her death, when her family went through her things, that she became famous."

Graham nodded. He also knew of Clara's history. He thought it was sad that such a great artist as she was had hidden her talent. Hardly anyone knew about her until the beginning of the twentieth century. He wondered if she regretted not moving on with her life after Marcus left. To him, it was sad that she had pinned for him all these years.

"So your agency is collecting all of Clara's paintings? Can you just take them now? Wouldn't that stop the time-travel problem?"

Graham smiled. "If only it could be that easy. No. They need to be finished. I can't change history."

"Of course. Trying to stop these devices from changing history seems to be your biggest goal," Destiny said dryly.

"It's the most important aspect of it all."

Destiny stood. "This rock is getting a bit hard." She grinned at him and then started to walk along the ocean shore. Graham got up and followed behind her. Every few steps, Destiny would bend and pick up a shell, inspect it, and then drop it to the ground. Graham enjoyed watching her.

He had gone on many time-travel jobs and had met many people, but none of them had made an impression on him like Destiny had. There was just something about her that drew him to her. He had never had that happen before. The war had changed everything, and he had been so busy learning how to live and survive in his new world, having a girlfriend wasn't at the top of his list. He dated some for fun, but whenever the woman started to indicate she wanted their friendship to develop into something more, he quickly ended things.

But Destiny was different. There was something about her that drew him to her, and he wasn't sure he liked it, especially because once he dropped her off in 2017 and collected Clara's painting, he would never see her again. He was from 2045 after all.

At one point, Destiny stopped and faced the ocean. She closed her eyes and lifted her face to the sun, obviously enjoying the warmth. The wind blew a few wisps of hair that were escaping from the pins Clara had used across her face. Graham stepped next to her and brushed the hair from her face with his hand. Her eyes opened with surprise, and for a moment they looked at each other.

Graham moved his hand to the back of her head. "Clara did a fine job pinning your hair up, but I have to admit, I like your hair the way it was, hanging down, free." He started to remove the pins, dropping each one to the sand as he did so. Destiny seemed in a trance, allowing him to remove the pins until her hair was free of them. Graham ran his fingers through her hair. "You have beautiful hair."

Destiny still didn't say anything, but her eyes shone with happiness. Graham knew he could keep moving forward if he wanted to, and he gathered her into his arms. As she settled against him, he felt her sigh, and he knew she was feeling the same emotions he was. Instead of speaking, he cupped her face with both hands and lowered his mouth to hers. Stars seemed to explode around them.

After a moment, Destiny stepped back, her eyes wide in disbelief, a hand touching her mouth. Graham wanted to pull her back to him and finish the kiss, but he knew it wouldn't be wise to do so.

Destiny was having a hard time believing what just happened. She had never had such a reaction with another man who had kissed her before, although admittedly, she had only had two boyfriends in her lifetime. She had a hard time trusting herself with her feelings when she was around men because of her gift. When she had any type of physical contact with a man, it was hard to block their emotions as well as hers, and it was easier to just pull away.

She distinctly remembered one man she had met while she was in college. She had done her best to block any of his feelings she might have felt. Things became serious between them very quickly, in a matter of months, and Destiny had started to let herself fall for him. One night he had come to her apartment upset. He had refused to tell her what was wrong, but in her attempt to console him, she accidently let her guard down. She immediately found out, through the negative energy that was radiating from him, that he was married and had just had a fight with his wife. Destiny had immediately ended the relationship and promised herself that never again would she allow herself to trust another man. Months later, she had realized that her gift had protected her from even more hurt. But now, even though she had only just met Graham, she was starting to realize that he was different, that things could be different between them. He seemed to understand her. Did she dare let herself trust him?

She looked at Graham to see what he was thinking and immediately realized that he was blocking his own emotions from her. He broke the silence, as if the kissed hadn't just happened.

"Why don't we ask Clara to show us her paintings?" Graham suggested. "Maybe we can figure out what is making them into time-travel devices."

Destiny nodded her agreement as she bent to pick up the hairpins that had dropped to the sand. Her heart was heavy that Graham seemed to want to ignore the feelings between them, but she also knew that it very likely was just as well.

As they walked up the dirt path towards the cottage, Destiny knew she could easily fall in love with Graham. She now understood what Clara meant when she talked about her connection to Marcus. Once a person feels that strong bond with someone else, it would be very hard to settle for less. She thought about Graham's description of his time. She knew deep inside that even though there was an obvious connection between them, nothing could ever happen. They weren't from the same time period.

Chapter Nine

When the cottage came into view, Graham stopped and looked at her. "I think we need to return to your time as soon as possible."

Destiny hesitated, but she then nodded her agreement. "That would probably be a good idea. I'm sure Aurora is wondering what happened. I have no idea what I will tell her."

"I think you will find that she will be very understanding," Graham said with a grin.

Destiny looked at him confusion. "What do you mean?"

"Let's just say she has had experience with time travel herself."

"Oh, really?" Destiny questioned with interest. "What happened? Where did she go? What device did she use?"

"I'll let her tell you her story, if she chooses to," Graham replied.

Destiny wanted to argue, but she decided that it was only fair to Aurora to ask her instead of insisting that Graham tell her. She was very curious, though. It was obvious that Graham was telling the truth, that time travel was much more common than most people believed.

"How are we going to get back to my time?" Destiny asked instead. "The painting that brought me here isn't finished yet, so I assume that we can't use that route. How did you get here?"

Graham held out his arm and pointed to a watch. "We will use this."

"A watch?" Destiny asked as she leaned closer to him to inspect it. "It looks like an antique old-fashioned watch."

The watch had the usual type of face on it, showing the time and date. It looked like it was at least one-hundred-years old. She had seen similar ones in old black and white photographs. But there were a number of very small buttons along its edges. Graham took his hand and covered it for a moment. The face of the watch disappeared, and it suddenly looked like her own smart watch with a small blank screen.

"How does it work?" she questioned with fascination.

"I use these buttons to control where I go. I can input the exact time, year and location. Then I use this button here to transport me." He continued to explain the purpose of all the buttons. One of them was used to travel to the location he wanted. Another was used to return him to his own time. A small button was like a GPS and recorded every place he went to. Another one was a voice recognition button that he used to journal exactly what he did for each job.

"The watch was made to stay on my wrist at all times. I can't take it off, unless it's deactivated," Graham continued to explain. "When it's time for us to return to 2017, we will need to hold hands. I will push this button, and we will be gone."

"That's really neat. It looks like a fancy version of my smartwatch." She wished she could show Graham her own watch that she had purchased for herself on her birthday, but she had left it at home.

Graham nodded. "I think this watch is based on what smart watches are in your time, just improved."

"What about charging it?" Destiny asked, thinking about how she had to charge her watch quite often. The battery only lasted about a day. Because of that reason, she often forgot to put it on.

"The battery lasts over a month. When it does need to be charged, all I need to do is allow the sun to shine on it for a few seconds. The sun immediately charges the battery, and it's good to go."

"Things have definitely improved between 2017 and 2045," Destiny said, grinning. She had a small solar panel that she had bought in order to charge her phone if she ever needed to if the electricity went out, but it took all day to charge something, and it had to be out in the sun the entire time.

Graham held out his hand. "Let's go ask Clara to show us her paintings."

Destiny gladly slipped her hand in his. "Are we going to tell her that her paintings end up being time-travel devices?"

Graham shook his head. "There isn't any reason to tell her that. I would like to try to figure out what she is using or doing to make them that way, though."

"If you figure it out, will you stop her from doing it?"

He shook his head. "No, because..."

"It will change history," Destiny finished for him, laughing.

When they entered the cottage, Clara looked up from where she was sitting, a small book in her lap. She looked at their clasped hands and smiled.

"It seems that you had a nice walk," she commented, looking pleased.

"We did," Destiny said, flushing a bit. Graham squeezed her hand, and she knew he wanted her to bring up the subject of the paintings.

"Clara, last night before Graham showed up, I couldn't sleep. I have to admit that I did a bit of snooping."

"What do you mean?" Clara asked, puzzled.

"I looked around your painting room last night," Destiny confessed.

Clara sighed. At first Destiny thought she looked upset, but then she laughed.

"I thought I heard someone in that room."

"Would you be willing to show us your paintings?" Graham asked.

Clara looked surprised. "Why would you want to see them? I'm really not very good. Most of them aren't even finished. I have a bad habit of starting a painting but then not finishing them."

"I think what you have completed is beautiful," Destiny told her honestly.

Clara didn't look like she believed her, but she set the book she was holding aside and stood. "Well, if you would like to see them, I will show them to you."

Destiny and Graham followed Clara up the stairs. As she opened the door, Destiny could smell the odor of paints in the air. They waited patiently while Clara opened the curtains to allow natural light into the room.

Just like Destiny had seen the night before, there was an easel standing near the window, with a small table and chair beside it. Along two of the walls were stacks of canvases. Most of them were of half-finished paintings. They were all of landscapes, mostly of the ocean or other places nearby. There was a finished portrait of a young girl hanging on her wall, but the rest of the walls were empty.

"Can I look through these canvases?" Graham asked curiously.

"Of course, but I'm still not sure why you want to see them. Like I said, they really aren't very good."

"Let me be the judge of that," Graham told her with a grin.

For the next few minutes, Destiny and Graham looked through the stacks of canvases. Destiny loved what she saw. Clara was actually very good, and she wished she could convey that to her.

"What made you start painting?" Graham asked.

"I showed interest when I was young, and my father made sure I received lessons."

"So you have been painting your entire life?"

"Yes. I have very little to occupy my time, so I spend it painting or working in my flower gardens."

"Have you sold any?" Destiny asked, even though she knew the answer to that question.

Clara looked surprised at her question. "No one would be really interested in purchasing my paintings. They are mostly dabbling. I have given a few away as gifts, but that is about it."

"Can you explain what your process is? Where do you get the paints? What type do you use?"

"I purchase most of my paints at a store that is located near London. I only go there once a year though. I've made some of my paints with dyes from the flowers I grow." Clara pointed to a small, gray bottle. "This pigment is from some of the rocks I've found by the ocean."

As Destiny continued to look through each of Clara's paintings, Clara continued to explain her process. She looked around carefully but couldn't see anything that would be making the paintings become time-travel devices.

"I have to give most of the credit to why I paint to Marcus," Clara said. "He really encouraged me to paint and insisted I have the time to 'develop my talent,' as he called it. He even gave me a set of brushes to use. They are much better quality brushes than I've ever been able to find. I have no idea where he got them."

Destiny and Graham looked at each other. "Can I see them?" Graham asked.

Clara walked over to a table that held most of her paints and picked up a few brushes. "When he first gave them to me, there were five of them. But two of them fell apart with use. I only have three left. I am very selective as to when I use them." She handed them to Graham.

Destiny watched as Graham looked them over carefully and then handed them back to Clara. "They do look like good brushes."

"Do you…" Clara said and then hesitated as she looked at Graham. "Do you think Marcus could have brought them from his time?"

Graham shrugged his shoulders, but Destiny could tell he thought the same. "Could be."

They spent an hour in Clara's painting room. Destiny asked Clara many questions about each painting. At first, Clara would answer the questions with as few words as possible. She soon relaxed as she realized Destiny and Graham were genuinely interested in her work, and she began to open up.

Each painting had a history behind it. Some were from Clara's childhood. Others were landscapes of when she went on trips with her family. Finally, Destiny asked about the portrait of the young girl that hung on the wall.

"That's Katherine," Clara said sadly. "My sister gave me a small likeness of her. It is the only thing I have of her. I repainted the likeness into a larger painting."

Destiny desperately wished she could somehow help Clara find peace about what happened with her daughter. "She is beautiful."

Clara walked across the room until she stood beside the portrait. "She has some of my features. She has Marcus's hair."

Destiny noticed that Katherine had dark red hair. Her smile was mischievous, as if she was about to start laughing. Clara had painted her sitting on a bench surrounded by flowers. A few birds were in the trees, and a butterfly fluttered by Katherine's hand near a beautiful red rose she was holding.

"Clara," Graham said and waited until the woman looked at him. "Marcus was right to encourage your painting. Finish the ones you've started. You have a gift. Share it."

Clara smiled. "Thank you for your encouragement." She looked at them both. "You are planning to leave soon for your time, aren't you?"

Graham nodded.

"It's almost dinner time. At least eat before you leave."

"We can do that," Graham agreed with a smile.

Clara prepared a delicious meal of roast beef, potatoes, gravy, and fresh garden-peas. Conversation during dinner was light-hearted and fun. After the meal was over, Destiny insisted on doing the dishes and proceeded to wash them exactly how Clara had done it the day before. She was proud of herself for remembering how to shave the bar of soap into the hot water. Graham helped by drying the dishes and putting them away.

After the dishes were done, Destiny went up to the room she had used and quickly changed into her own clothing. When she went back down the stairs to join Graham, she noticed he had his backpack with him, and he had changed into his own clothing as well.

"Don't forget this," Clara said, as she gave Destiny the book *Pride and Prejudice* she had purchased for her.

"Oh, I definitely don't want to forget that," Destiny breathed, as she took the book. "Thank you so much."

"I wish I could persuade you to stay longer, but I know it wouldn't be wise to be gone longer than you need to be. I've enjoyed your visit," Clara said, as she gave them each a hug.

"I've also enjoyed it," Destiny said. "I'm so glad I was able to meet you."

Graham looked anxious to be gone, so Destiny turned to him, expecting him to set his watch, so they could leave. But what he did next surprised her.

"Clara, remember. You have some paintings to finish," he told the older woman who nodded her head that she would. "It's been a joy to meet you." He turned to Destiny. "I think it would be best if we went down to the ocean to leave."

"Okay," Destiny agreed.

After exchanging goodbyes and hugs one more time with Clara, Destiny and Graham left and walked down to the shore. Destiny looked back once, and she could see the older woman standing in the exact spot they had left her, watching them.

"Is it always this hard to leave the people you meet when you time travel?" Destiny asked, feeling sad that they needed to leave.

Graham shook his head. "Most of the time I have very little interaction with the people I meet. I am supposed to leave as little an impression on people as possible."

Destiny thought about when she had first met Graham. It would have worked out that way, if she hadn't touched the painting that had brought her through time. Graham would have just been another customer to her. She would have remembered the sparks that had traveled between them when he'd run into her, but she would have quickly forgotten about him. But now her entire life had changed, all because of a beautiful painting of a cottage tucked near an English village by the sea.

When they arrived at the beach, Graham turned to her. "Are you ready?"

"Yes."

Graham held out his hand, and Destiny grasped it with her own, squeezing tightly. Still holding her hand, Graham pushed one of the buttons on his watch. And they were gone.

Chapter Ten

J ust like that, they were standing in Aurora's art gallery. It was getting dark and Destiny could tell Aurora had already closed it for the day. She felt a bit dizzy and closed her eyes, waiting for it to pass.

"Do you get dizzy like this all the time?"

Graham smiled. "I did at first, but I've gotten used to it."

Destiny watched as he glanced at the very painting that started their whole adventure. Suddenly she didn't want him to leave, not yet.

"Do you have to leave for your time right now?" Destiny asked him.

Graham hesitated. "I really should. My boss is probably wondering what happened. This trip was supposed to be an easy one. I should have been back the day after I arrived here."

Destiny opened her mouth, ready to argue with him. What could she say to convince him to stay for awhile longer?

"But, since it's already almost dark, I don't think it would hurt to stay the night. I'll leave in the morning. I really should make arrangements to purchase this painting from Aurora. It wouldn't be good to just have it disappear."

At his words, Destiny's heart soared. She instantly knew he was as reluctant to leave her as she was for him to go.

"Why don't you come to my apartment?" Destiny invited him. "I have a fold out bed you can sleep on. We can go out for breakfast in the morning before the gallery opens."

Graham agreed with her idea. They left the gallery, and Destiny made sure it was locked securely behind her. She walked to the place where she had left her car and breathed a sigh of relief that it was still there. They climbed in and soon were on their way to her apartment.

2045, early morning

Trystan set down his phone in frustration. Where was Graham? He knew that their boss had given him a job of collecting a *Clara Moore* painting, but it should have only taken no more than a day. It had now been three. Did something happen?

There were always risks with time travel. When Jack gave them a job to do, intense research was always done before they left. Mistakes were avoided most of the time, but they did still happen on occasion.

He started to dial his boss's phone number but then decided to go talk to him personally. Leaving his office, he informed his secretary that he would be gone for a few minutes and where to find him, if needed. With large strides, he took the stairs down to the bottom floor. He walked outside and headed towards the large building that was headquarters.

Once he entered the building and let the security guy know who he wanted to see, he was soon knocking on Jack's door.

"Come in," he heard, as he swung the door open.

"Trystan," Jack boomed. "What can I do for you?"

Trystan studied Jack for a moment, taking in his small, stocky stature and full head of white hair. He wondered how such a small man could have such a loud voice.

"I wanted to see if you had heard from my brother."

"Graham?" Jack shook his head. "Can't say I have."

"He hasn't returned from the last job you sent him on," Trystan informed him, even though he knew Jack was already aware of that fact.

"I wouldn't worry about him."

"Don't you think you should at least track where he is? What if he ran into some kind of trouble?"

"He hasn't sent an SOS out, so I assume he is fine," Jack stated, talking about how their watches had a button that agents could push if they got into any kind of trouble.

"I would like permission to travel to the year and location he is supposed to be in and make sure he is okay," Trystan said.

Jack studied Trystan with a bit of sympathy in his eyes. Trystan knew his boss was aware of their history. Graham was the only family he had left after *The Terrible War*. Trystan always seemed to panic when he didn't know where his brother was.

"Let's give him until later today," Jack finally suggested. "If he isn't back by late afternoon, we'll track him, and you can go after him, if needed."

Trystan opened his mouth to argue, but he knew that once Jack made up his mind about something, nothing would change it. He hesitated before nodding his head reluctantly.

"Alright. Late afternoon then."

He turned on his heel to leave, but Jack stopped him. "I'm sure Graham is fine, Trystan."

Trystan didn't say anything, but he waited to be dismissed.

"Some of the other agents have returned with new time-travel devices. They need to be cataloged at the warehouse. Why don't you spend some time there, doing that?"

Trystan wanted to glare at him, but in the end, he nodded his head in agreement and then left the office. He knew why Jack gave him the job of cataloging. It would keep him busy until Graham returned.

2017

Once Destiny and Graham arrived at her apartment, they spent some time getting his bed ready for him to sleep in. Graham sat at her kitchen table doing work on his portable pocket computer. It was as small as her tablet, but more powerful than the largest computer that was available in the current year. Destiny watched in amazement, as he gave commands to the phone, and the information he wanted appeared on what looked like an invisible screen just above his wrist. He typed a few things in what looked like a word document before closing it. Throughout the drive to her apartment and the time they spent after arriving, a plan formed in Destiny's mind. As she watched Graham work on his small computer, she became more determined to make sure her plan worked.

Destiny went through her own email and voicemail, returning messages. After she was finished, she found her favorite ice cream in the freezer and prepared two bowls for them both. She set one of them down beside Graham, who smiled his thanks. Destiny sat in the chair across from him and prepared to put her plan in action.

"I want to go with you when you leave for your time," Destiny announced, doing her best to keep her voice level and matter-of-fact. But deep inside, she was shaking like a leaf.

Graham didn't even look at her. He took a bite of ice cream and swallowed it before answering. "No."

Destiny continued as if Graham hadn't spoken. "I will only stay a few days. We've seen what life was like in Clara's time. You know what it's like in 2017. Now that I know time travel is possible, I would like to see what 2045 is like."

"Definitely not. It's out of the question. Just get this idea out of your head."

"Why?" Destiny asked with frustration. She had known he was not going to like her idea, but she didn't think he'd be so against it. What about the kiss they had shared? Maybe it had meant nothing to him. He probably kissed all sorts of beautiful women, as he traveled to different times.

"If you come with me, it would change history."

Destiny shrugged. She was starting to get tired of that reason Graham always gave when he didn't want to tell her anything. "I think we've already changed history, don't you think?"

"Traveling back to Clara's time couldn't be helped. I cannot take you back with me. I know you are curious about what your future entails. I would be if I were in your shoes. But it is out of the question."

"Wanting to go with you is more than just curiosity," Destiny admitted, trying to let him know that she wanted to spend more time with him. She knew nothing could come of any type of relationship with him. After all, he was from the future. But she wanted to spend as much time with him as possible.

"My job is to collect time-travel devices, nothing more," Graham insisted.

"What about just for one day?"

Graham sighed and closed his computer and slid it into his jacket pocket. "Do you realize how much trouble I'm going to be in because I went after you to begin with?"

Destiny's eyes narrowed in confusion. "Why would you be in trouble?"

"Protocol dictates that, instead of following you to Clara's cottage, I should have taken the painting back to my time and should have explained the problem to my boss. He in turn would have thought about it for a few days before deciding whether you should be returned to your own time or not. I took matters into my own hands and went after you."

"Well, I, for one, am glad you did. I would not have been happy if I were stuck in 1879."

Graham gave her a small grin before continuing. "Protocol dictates that on every job I'm given, I only bring back the device, no people. If I brought you, I could be fired."

Destiny didn't want Graham to be fired, and she frowned. There had to be a way to keep spending time with him. She didn't want to put him out of a job, but she couldn't just let him go.

"What about…" Destiny started to suggest, but Graham got to his feet.

"I've decided that it isn't a good idea that I stay here this evening. I am going to leave now. I will see you in the morning."

Before Destiny could say anything, he picked up his backpack and opened the door to her apartment.

"But where are you going to go?" Destiny asked, but she was talking to herself. He had already left.

Graham left Destiny's apartment with a banging of the door. He was aware that he needed to cool down and knew it wouldn't be smart to stay the night. He would stay in the same park he had before, under the large pine tree. Swinging his backpack on his shoulders, he headed down the street. He wasn't exactly sure where he was, so he programmed his watch to find the park and breathed a sigh of relief when he realized it wasn't too far away.

He felt bad for arguing with Destiny. He had really enjoyed getting to know her over the last few days. He didn't regret going after her when he realized the painting had sent her back in time. He only hoped his boss would understand. He knew he could have taken Destiny back to her time the moment he had arrived on Clara's beach, but in a weak moment, he allowed himself to be talked into staying overnight. She seemed to have caused quite a few weak moments for him.

The wind started to pick up, and Graham pulled the collar of his jacket up around his neck. He hoped it wasn't going to storm. It would be a very uncomfortable night for him if it started to rain. But even the threat of a storm didn't stop Graham from continuing forward and away from Destiny's apartment.

Once he found the park, he spent the next few hours walking around, waiting until it became too dark for anyone to see him. The entire time, he couldn't stop thinking about Destiny. He had never been so attracted to a woman as he was to Destiny. He was thirty-five years old, but he had never been interested in settling down with one woman. He had spent his teenage years just trying to survive through *The Terrible War*. Then the years after it were spent trying to recover, working hard to help rebuild his city and neighborhood. He had also spent one of those years looking for his family before realizing that only his younger brother, Trystan, had survived.

Since he had been promoted to a *Time-Travel Guardian*, he loved his job. He felt he had the perfect way to support himself. But his boss always insisted that family had no place in the Agency. Graham knew of a few men who had been removed from the Agency when they married and started a family of their own. Although he had to admit to himself, he wasn't sure if his boss had immediately had them removed, or if the agents had requested the change on their own.

But what was he thinking? Nothing could ever happen between him and Destiny. She lived in 2017. Ironically, he knew she had been born before he had by about twenty years. As he quickly did the math in his head, he knew she had been born in 1990. He had been born in the year 2010. She had no idea what her future held, the terrible destruction that was going to happen in less than eight years in her time. And he knew he needed to keep it that way. He admitted to himself that when Destiny asked to go with him to his time, part of him was tempted. But it was out of the question. He felt bad he had left her so abruptly, not even saying goodbye. He would be at the gallery as soon as it opened the next morning. He would be able to say goodbye then. He hoped she wouldn't be too angry with him.

Chapter Eleven

The next morning, Destiny woke up the moment it started to get light. She had slept hardly at all through the night, feeling a deep regret for her argument with Graham. Regardless of the fact that she wanted to go with him to his time, she knew she shouldn't have pushed the issue. She understood why he had refused to take her. It would change history, hers and his. And what if she couldn't get back to 2017? She just wished he hadn't been so stern about it. His reaction to her idea made her realize that he really didn't feel anything for her, even though they had shared the most wonderful kiss she had ever experienced in her twenty-seven years.

He probably kisses every woman he meets up with on his travels through time, Destiny muttered to herself.

Destiny pushed her blankets away and climbed from her bed. She wasn't due at the gallery until after lunch, but she wanted to be there when it opened. She knew Graham would show up to get the painting as soon as he could, and she at least wanted to say goodbye. She also knew she needed to talk to Aurora, although she had no idea what she was going to tell her. She definitely wanted to get to work before her boss, though. She knew Graham would leave as soon as he retrieved the painting. He wasn't going to wait around for her if she wasn't there.

After showering and putting on her favorite flowered skirt and pink shirt, she quickly made herself a simple breakfast. Soon she was on her way to the gallery. When she arrived, she parked in her usual spot, and her heart skipped a beat when she saw Graham leaning against the window, his backpack at his feet. She couldn't help but admire his good looks. Did all men from the future look so handsome? He hadn't noticed her arrival yet. He was looking off in the distance, almost as if he was remembering something. Was he comparing his Denver in 2045 to hers in 2017? It was too weird to think about.

Destiny got out of her car and slammed the door, and Graham looked over at her. His eyes became unreadable, but he walked toward her.

"Hello," Destiny said, when he was close enough to hear her. "I hope you found a place to sleep."

"I did, thank you. It was fine. I was just glad it didn't rain."

Destiny was confused at his statement, but she decided to ignore it. "I know you want to get the painting and leave as soon as you can. But I want to say something first."

Graham didn't say anything. He kept looking at her with a peculiar look in his eyes, as if he were expecting her to continue their argument.

"I'm sorry I started that argument last night. I'm just curious about your time. I understand why you don't want me to go with you."

Graham's eyes cleared, as if in relief. "I have enjoyed getting to know you."

"I just wish you could tell me something about the future. Give me a hint of what's to come," Destiny teased, knowing he wouldn't say anything.

Graham's face became very serious. "I can tell you this. Keep a backpack with you with at least three-days' ration of ready-to-eat meals and a few emergency supplies. When the time comes, go deep into the mountains."

Destiny felt confused at his words. "What do you mean?"

He shook his head. "That's all I can say. You will know what I mean when the time comes."

She looked at him quizzically before deciding she would think about what he had just advised her later. "I guess I'll open the door."

Graham stood to the side and waited as Destiny used her key to open the door. Once they were inside, she turned on the lights, as she walked to the back room. She could smell coffee brewing and knew Aurora was already there. Her boss was most likely doing paperwork.

"You are here early," Aurora noted, as she looked up from her desk, her long hair spilling down her back.

Destiny noticed that Aurora was looking at her quizzily, and she waited for the questions: where had she been for the last two days, and why did she leave the gallery without saying something to her? But the questions didn't come, and Destiny decided she would come up with something to tell Aurora after Graham left.

"Yes, we have someone who is interested in the *Clara Moore* painting," Destiny explained. She thought it strange that Aurora was acting like Destiny hadn't been gone at all.

"Is this customer here now?"

Destiny nodded. "He's in the showroom."

Aurora stood gracefully and walked into the large room where most of the merchandise was displayed. Destiny watched as her boss basically floated towards where Graham was standing, and Destiny smiled to herself. She had never seen Aurora move too fast or too slow. She always seemed to glide from one place to another.

"So, are you the person who is interested in my *Clara Moore* painting?" Aurora asked, as she held out her hand for Graham to shake.

"Yes, ma'am," Graham said, as he glanced between Aurora and Destiny. "I would like to purchase it."

Destiny discreetly rolled her eyes. She knew Graham would be taking the painting whether Aurora sold it to him or not. She waited for Aurora to tell him it wasn't for sell.

"May I ask why you are so interested in this particular painting?" Aurora asked, as she waved her arm in a large circle. "After all, there are plenty more paintings in this room alone that are for sell."

"Let's just say my boss has been looking for this painting for quite some time and is willing to pay you what it's worth."

Aurora studied Graham for a moment and then turned her back and walked into the small room where the painting was located. Graham and Destiny followed her, and the three of them studied it for a moment. Destiny wondered if she reached out to touch it, if she would again be transported back to Clara's time. She slipped her hands into the pockets of her full skirt, so she wouldn't be tempted to touch it herself.

"I have always felt there is something interesting about this painting," Aurora commented. "It's almost as if there is some sort of... power associated with it." Aurora continued to look at the painting and then turned to look at Graham. "Am I right?"

Destiny stared at Aurora in amazement. Was she aware that the painting's power was time travel?

"I can't say, ma'am," Graham told her.

Aurora waved her hand. "Please don't call me ma'am. It makes me feel...old."

Graham nodded once in agreement.

"I'm sure you are aware of how much this painting is worth," Aurora continued.

"My boss is willing to pay you for what it's worth."

Aurora didn't respond for a long time. Destiny looked at the painting very carefully, as if she was memorizing all the features – the thatched roof, red trim, flower gardens, and the sea in the background. And it looked to her like the hawk had moved... again.

"I will sell it to you for what I paid for it," Aurora announced.

Again, Destiny was shocked. She remembered the day Aurora brought the painting into the gallery. She specifically told Destiny that it wasn't for sale and never would be. When Destiny asked her why she was keeping it in the gallery if she didn't intend to sell it, she told her she needed to keep an eye on it.

Graham didn't say anything at first and Destiny wished she could know what he was thinking, what Aurora was thinking. As the two stared at each other, she could almost swear they were somehow communicating.

"Thank you," Graham finally said.

Over the next few minutes, Graham made arrangements to purchase the painting. Destiny quietly watched as he pulled a credit card out of his backpack, and she smiled. Obviously, the people in the future still used credit cards. When the last paper was signed, Aurora offered to wrap it for Graham, but he declined.

"I can take care of it," he told her.

Aurora smiled and then started to leave the room. At the entrance, she stopped and looked at Destiny.

"Destiny. Be careful with your choices."

Destiny looked at Aurora in confusion. What was she talking about? Before she could ask, her boss disappeared into her office, closing the door behind her.

What was that all about? Destiny stared at the closed door for a moment before turning to Graham. She noticed he already had the painting off the wall and had leaned it against the wall. His backpack was back on his back and he was punching information in his watch.

"Are you leaving now?" Destiny asked, her voice shaking a bit.

Graham nodded. "I need to get back. I was not supposed to be gone as long as I have, remember?"

"Are you going to leave without saying goodbye?"

Graham's eyes softened. "Of course not." He glanced at the painting, almost as if he was expecting the painting to disappear. Then he walked towards her.

"I've enjoyed getting to know you," Graham said. "This trip wasn't supposed to turn out the way it did, but I'm glad I was able to meet you."

"Well, if I had to travel back in time, I'm glad I did it with you," Destiny said with a smile.

They looked at each other for a long moment. Suddenly Destiny was in his arms, and she had no idea how she got there. Again, Graham cupped her face with his hands and placed his lips on hers. And again, stars exploded around them. Destiny suddenly understood why Clara never remarried after Marcus left her. Once a woman meets her soulmate, no one else can replace him. Then Graham stepped back.

"Goodbye," Graham said to her, after placing another kiss on her cheek.

Destiny refused to say goodbye back to him. As Graham picked up the picture with one hand, she knew what she had to do. It wasn't something she should do. She *had* to do it. She *had* to go with him. When he pushed the button on his watch, he closed his eyes, and Destiny saw him start to disappear. As fast as she could, she jumped on him, wrapping her legs around his waist, her arms around him. They flew through time, together.

Chapter Twelve

D estiny felt a sudden thump, as they both fell to the ground. She opened her eyes and realized she was still tangled up in Graham's arms. The painting was beside them.

"What do you think you are doing? Do you have any idea what trouble you just caused?" Graham yelled at her angrily. "You have to go back. Right now!"

"I don't know what I was thinking," Destiny stammered, trying to explain herself. How could she tell him that it was almost as if she *had* to come with him? That if she had not, her life wouldn't be the same ever again? "I... just needed to come."

"You have to go back," Graham yelled again as he jumped to his feet, pulling Destiny up with him.

He started to punch information into his watch. Destiny backed away from him. She was determined to not go back to her time, at least not yet. She was in Graham's time, and she was going to experience at least a little bit of it.

Graham growled, as he tapped his watch and then shook his arm. "Come on!"

Destiny watched him for a few seconds before looking around at her surroundings. His apartment was decorated simply, but everything looked very comfortable. She saw a large aquarium against a wall. The floor was polished wood with thick carpets on it. She forced her gaze away from her surroundings and watched Graham tap his watch.

"It won't work!" Graham exclaimed angrily, as he shook his arm one more time. "Now what am I going to do? I can't send you back without this watch."

She knew if she said anything, it would make him angrier, so she kept quiet. Even though Graham was definitely upset at what she had done, she knew he would soon calm down, at least she hoped he would. They spent the next hour in silence. At first Destiny sat on his couch, but eventually she couldn't help herself. She had to explore Graham's world. She stood and watched the fish in his aquarium for a moment before looking at everything in the main room. Graham had pretty much everything she had in her apartment, but everything looked much newer and...different. There weren't buttons on anything, and she finally decided that maybe things worked by touch instead of buttons. He had what looked like a fancy stereo and screenless television system that was built right into the wall. She wanted to start touching things and try to figure out how they worked, but she didn't dare.

"I need to get the painting to the warehouse and talk to my boss," Graham finally said, breaking the silence. "You will need to come with me. Maybe he can figure out what to do."

Destiny turned from where she was studying his entertainment center. "I'm sorry that you are so angry that I followed you here. But I don't regret it. I'm glad I'm here."

Maybe she would be able to describe to him why she felt she had to come before she needed to leave, but she didn't even know how to express it herself.

Graham's face softened as he looked at her. He opened his mouth as if he wanted to say something, but he then closed it. He picked up the painting and slid it into a black carrying case. He put his backpack in a closet and locked it, pocketing the key. The last thing he did was go into the kitchen and pulled out what looked like protein bars from a cupboard and handed one to Destiny. When he continued to hold out his hand, Destiny slid the bar into her skirt pocket and put her hand in his. Immediately a zing traveled through her arm to her heart. As he guided her out of his apartment, she knew she would never regret following him here.

Graham did his best to shove down the immense happiness he was feeling that Destiny was by his side. He had been very upset when he realized what she had done. Right when he had started to leave the gallery, he had felt a body grab onto his. He immediately knew it was Destiny, and she had clung to him like Velcro. Then they had arrived to their destination, tumbling onto his living-room floor, her hair covering his face.

He didn't know why his watch had stopped working so he couldn't send her back to her time, and he hoped there wasn't anything wrong with it. But now that she was here in his time, why not enjoy her company? He knew Jack would arrange for Destiny to return to 2017 as soon as possible. He dreaded the conversation he would be having with his boss very shortly, and he only hoped he still had a job.

He tried to walk quickly to his car, but slowed down as Destiny looked around, her eyes wide in amazement. He knew she was seeing his time and comparing it to hers. How could she not? He opened the right door of his car and helped Destiny inside. He walked around to the left side and climbed in. He started to punch some numbers into the car's computer and heard Destiny gasp.

"Where is the steering wheel?"

Graham grinned, as he started to enjoy showing off some of the things 2017 didn't have. "This is what's called a driverless car. No one has a car with a steering wheel anymore."

"How does it work? I've heard of what is called self-driving cars in my time, but there are still steering wheels to use, just in case the driver needs to take over."

Destiny was silent for a moment as the car backed out of the parking space and started down the street. "How do you keep from getting in an accident?"

"Actually, accidents rarely happen. This car sends signals to all of the other vehicles around it. They all work together to get us where we want to go."

"You still have traffic lights," Destiny commented, as they drove under one.

"They aren't the same as the ones in your time. They are also connected with the cars' computers. If you notice, there isn't a yellow light."

"There isn't," Destiny practically squealed. "This is soooo cool!"

Destiny watched in amazement as Graham's car maneuvered through the traffic. Everything operated so smoothly. All the cars drove at the same speed, slowing down and then speeding up when needed. When they came to another intersection, Graham's car slowed down and then stopped, allowing some other cars to go through, and then his car started up again. Too soon, they were pulling into a large complex with what looked like government buildings. Destiny would have wanted to keep going and drive around the city for a bit, but she knew that Graham wanted to get the painting to his boss as soon as possible.

Once the car was parked, Graham carried the black case with one hand and grasped her elbow to guide her with the other. He moved her along quickly and she wished he'd slow down, so she could look around.

"I would have thought there'd be flying cars by now," Destiny joked.

"They are in the works," Graham responded. "The larger cities do have a few of them, but they aren't too popular yet. They are very expensive to purchase, and most of us are still recovering financially from...."

"From what?" Destiny asked innocently.

"From something that you don't need to know about."

"Oh, something that happened in your past, but my future," Destiny guessed. She wanted to insist that he tell her, but something in his voice made her wonder if she really wanted to know, and she didn't want to irritate him more than she already had.

Graham stopped in front of an elevator and pushed the up button.

"At least some things are still the same," Destiny said, gesturing to the elevator.

"Not everything has changed."

The doors opened and once inside, Graham pushed the button to floor fifteen. Destiny noticed it was the highest floor. The elevator zoomed up and within seconds they reached their destination. Obviously, Graham's time still had elevators, but they were much faster. He grabbed her hand as the doors opened, and soon he was opening up a fancy glass door.

"I'm here to see Jack McGee," Graham told the secretary.

"He's expecting you. Go ahead and go in," the woman informed him.

"Thank you."

Graham kept Destiny's hand in his and led them both through a closed door. An older man looked up at their entrance.

"Graham," the man stood, as he greeted him with a handshake. "I see you made it back safe and sound. Your brother was worried."

Graham's eyes narrowed a bit at his boss's words, and Destiny tucked this new information in the back of her mind.

"This is Destiny Goodman. Destiny, this is my boss, Jack McGee."

"It's good to meet you," Destiny said with a smile. She suddenly felt very nervous, as she realized she was meeting another man from the future. She noticed that Mr. McGee was shorter than the average man. She expected Graham's boss would be intimidating, but when he looked at her with a twinkle in his eyes, she instantly felt calmer.

"Sit down. Sit down, both of you," Mr. McGee invited. Once they were seated, he continued. "I expected you back within a day with the painting. I assume something happened to delay your return."

"The painting is right here," Graham said, as he passed the black case over the desk to his boss.

"Good, good," Mr. McGee said, with pleasure in his voice. He carefully unzipped the case and lifted the painting out. "Beautiful, beautiful."

"All of Clara Moore's paintings are beautiful," Destiny said.

Mr. McGee looked at her for a moment and then at Graham. "I would like to hear a report of how you recovered it. Shall I ask my secretary to take Destiny to the cafe?"

Graham glanced at her. "She's part of the story."

"Hmmm, interesting, interesting." He looked at her again as if he were trying to figure something out. Destiny did her best to not squirm under his scrutiny. "Well, let's hear it then."

Graham took a deep breath and started to talk. Destiny listened, as he told Mr. McGee everything that happened. He talked about how he had arrived in 2017 and had headed right to the gallery to collect the painting. He had discovered he needed to wait until the next day, so he had spent the night under a pine tree in the local park. He explained how Destiny had accidentally sent herself back through time when she touched the painting and how he went after her. He talked about having met Clara Moore and getting to know her. When Graham got to the part where he was ready to travel back to his own time with the painting, he didn't tell Mr. McGee how Destiny had grabbed onto him at the last second, traveling with him to 2045. In fact, Destiny noticed that he didn't put any of the blame on her whatsoever for anything that had happened between them.

Destiny looked at her hands, which were clasped in her lap when she realized this. He could have easily blamed all of it on her, and he didn't. At that moment, she realized she had fallen in love with him, and she didn't know what to do about it.

"Well, young lady," Mr. McGee started to say after Graham finished his story, but stopped. Destiny found herself under his scrutiny again, and she wondered what he was trying to see in her. This time, instead of trying not to squirm, she looked squarely back at him. Whatever he saw in her eyes must have satisfied him, for he nodded before continuing. "I'm guessing you couldn't resist the opportunity to see the future."

Destiny shrugged her shoulders, but she couldn't help but smile at him.

"Believe it or not, I understand, too well I'm afraid. Time travel can be fun, and it also can be addicting. But it can also be very dangerous, especially when this knowledge falls into the wrong hands. Because of these people, our government formed this secret agency. Our job is to find all the time-travel devices in the world, in all the different time-periods. We either collect them and bring them back here to our warehouse, or we shut them down."

"Graham told me a bit about it," Destiny admitted. "I promise that the first time I traveled through time, it was an accident."

"And the second time?"

Destiny smiled softly, as she shook her head and admitted, "It wasn't an accident that time."

"Tell me about Clara Moore," he requested.

Destiny's eyes lit up. "She is a wonderful woman. As you know, we went back to the year 1879. This was before her paintings became famous. She has a cute little cottage she lives in near the ocean."

"She lives alone?"

Destiny nodded. "Yes. She seems happy enough, but I do think she's a bit lonely. She welcomed us with open arms. I showed up first, and she instantly knew I was from the future. She didn't seem shocked at all. Then when Graham appeared, she invited us to spend the night. She hasn't always been alone, you know."

"What makes you say that?"

"She talked about a man named Marcus who came to her years ago. He was from the future, 1943 I think she said. They even married, but then he disappeared soon after."

"He disappeared? What did she think happened to him?"

"He probably somehow traveled back to his time and couldn't return."

Graham cleared his throat. "We saw the room that she created her paintings in. Most of them weren't finished. This one was there, only it was half finished. I encouraged her to finish them."

"Good, good. We shouldn't change history even though some of her paintings have become time-travel devices." He touched the one in front of him.

"It's too bad they have to be hidden away," Destiny commented. "Clara is a very talented artist."

"Yes. Yes, she is." Mr. McGee stared off into space for a moment.

"I do wish her husband could have stayed with her, or at least taken her with him. After all she was..." Destiny stopped talking, not sure if she should talk about her baby or not.

"She was what, young lady? Tell me," Mr. McGee ordered, his eyes that had been twinkling through the conversation so far now narrowed at her.

"She was pregnant."

"Pregnant?" Mr. McGee practically thundered, which seemed out of place coming from such a small man.

"She had a daughter," Graham broke into the conversation. "She didn't raise her. Her sister talked her into giving her the child. She raised her as her own."

"Oh, no," Mr. McGee breathed, and suddenly he was very pale.

He looked so upset, Destiny instantly wanted to get up and give him a hug. What was so upsetting about their story? It was sad, but after all, technically Clara Moore was dead now, as well as her daughter.

"Are you okay, sir?" Destiny asked with concern.

"Yes, yes," he muttered, but he stood to his feet and started to pace behind his desk, his hands clasped behind his back. He started to talk to himself in a language Destiny had never heard before. She looked at Graham and could tell he was also confused and as concerned as she was. After a few minutes of pacing, he sat in his chair again, looking like he wasn't upset at all.

"Well, young lady, what are we going to do with you?" he asked her.

"I told her she needs to go back to 2017 as soon as possible. In fact, I tried to take her back, but my watch stopped working."

"The Ziran Watch? Interesting, interesting."

"As soon as it's fixed, I'll take her back."

Mr. McGee smiled at them both, letting his gaze linger on Destiny. "Don't be in such a hurry, Graham. There's not much you can do about it, now that she's here."

Chapter Thirteen

Destiny's heart jumped in her chest, as she just realized Mr. McGee was giving her permission to stay for awhile, and she had to force herself to not jump out of her chair and do a happy dance. She glanced at Graham who also looked shocked, but she knew his surprise was likely for a different reason. After all, he had been expecting Mr. McGee to be upset and to possibly fire him after everything that had happened. But in Destiny's eyes, Mr. McGee seemed much more understanding than Graham had originally made him out to be.

Suddenly there was a knock on the door. At Mr. McGee's command to enter, it burst open. A man who looked very similar to Graham came in, and Destiny instantly knew it was his younger brother.

"You are back," the man said, as the two gave each other a quick hug. "I'm glad to see you."

"See, Trystan? He's back safe and sound," Mr. McGee said with a grin at the two brothers.

Trystan noticed Destiny sitting next to Graham. "Introduce me, dear brother," he drawled.

Graham gave his brother a warning look. Trystan liked to flirt with any woman who even looked at him twice. Usually this never bothered him, but he suddenly found that he didn't like the idea that his brother might hit on Destiny.

"This is Destiny Goodman. When I traveled back to our time, I ended up with a passenger."

"Hi, Destiny. I'm Graham's brother. Can you see the resemblance?"

Destiny grinned at him, instantly charmed by the new arrival. "You do look similar."

And they did look quite a bit alike. They were the same height and weight. Trystan's hair was a little bit longer, but the same shade as Graham's. If Destiny had just met Trystan on the street, she would have thought he was Graham, except for the fact that Trystan had a long thin scar on the side of his right cheek, almost at the hairline, and she wondered how he had gotten it.

"It's nice to meet you," Destiny said.

"Likewise. So you are from 2017?" Trystan asked, but kept talking before Destiny could answer. "I remember that year, don't you, Graham? You would have been seven then and I was six. Remember those bikes Dad gave us for our birthdays? And you crashed yours on the first day you used it going down that big hill."

"Yeah. Dad made me continue to ride that bike to school, even though the handlebars were crooked, and I had a hard time making it go straight."

"It was good enough to get you to school. That's all that was important."

"Mom used to say that," Graham said quietly.

Destiny noted the sadness in his voice and remembered that he had said something about not having any family except a brother. Obviously, their parents were gone now.

Trystan turned to Destiny. "So what year were you born?"

"1990. I'm 27."

Trystan smirked at Graham. "Technically, she's older than you, brother."

"Enough of this," Mr. McGee broke in. "Graham, I'd like you to take this painting to the warehouse and catalog it. You know where to put it. I would like to study it, but it will be safer in the warehouse until I have time. As far as the problem with your watch, I think you will find it will fix itself in time. Trystan, I have a job for you. My secretary has the details."

"Will I be going on another job?" Graham asked.

"Not at the moment. You have a guest. Plus, didn't you ask to take a few days off after this job was completed?"

Graham shrugged. "The job took longer than planned. I'm okay with not taking any days off."

"I'm sure I won't be here for long. Then you can get back to work," Destiny commented, almost feeling hurt that he seemed to want to leave her so quickly.

Mr. McGee focused his attention on her, looking stern. "Destiny, I do feel I need to chastise you for coming here. Time travel is very dangerous if you don't know what you're doing. If you had let go of Graham for even a moment, you could have traveled to another location, and we might not have been able to find you. I admonish you to never try that again."

Destiny nodded. She understood what Mr. McGee was trying to say, although she still didn't regret what she had done.

"If...I mean when you return to your time, you must promise that you tell no one about your experiences, with Clara and with Graham."

Destiny shrugged, knowing this would be an easy promise to keep. "No one would believe me anyway."

"Do you promise? There will come a time when some will believe you."

Destiny nodded. "I promise."

But she noticed that Mr. McGee had said "if" before he corrected himself and said "when." Was there a chance she would be able to stay in 2045? Would Graham even want her to? Would she want to?

"I'll hold you to your word, then."

"I do understand what you are saying," Destiny reassured him.

"Good, good. Now then, Graham. Why don't you show Destiny around the *Shadow Works* compound? She can stay in one of the apartments we have for guests. After you drop the painting off at the warehouse, go ahead and take the rest of the day off. Take tomorrow off. Bring her into work the next day. Maybe she can be of some help."

Graham didn't say anything, but he nodded and stood, looking a little confused, yet relieved that the conversation was over. He quickly zipped up the case that carried the painting and picked it up. "I'll be in work the day after tomorrow at the usual time."

They left Mr. McGee's office, and Destiny waited while Graham briefly talked with the secretary. When they entered the elevator, Trystan stayed behind. Destiny assumed he was picking up the information for his next job. It was obvious Trystan had the same job Graham had, a Time-Travel Guardian collecting devices, and she wondered where he was going to next.

The elevator traveled down just as quickly. Once they were on the ground floor and outside, Graham helped her into what looked like a fancy golf cart. Graham drove this one instead of allowing it to move on its own, but he used a touch screen instead of a steering wheel. He drove slowly, acting as tour guide. She learned a lot about the place where Graham worked over the next few hours. The complex was called *Shadow Works Agency,* and it was located on the outskirts of Denver, covering ten-square acres of land. All of it was fenced and made secure as possible. The building they just left was in the middle of this large complex, and Graham called it the 'headquarters.' They turned right out of the parking lot and headed south. Just across from the headquarters was a full exercise gym, along with an Olympic-size pool (yes, they still had the Olympics in 2045), and a large game room. Next to the gym was the warehouse. Destiny was amazed at how large this building was, although it didn't look like a warehouse to her. It looked like a bunch of small business buildings connected together.

Graham took her inside, but they didn't stay long. She quietly watched as Graham logged into a wall computer and typed in a bunch of information about the painting. When he was done, he left Destiny alone while he went to another part of the warehouse. He wasn't gone very long.

"Are you done?" Destiny asked when he reappeared.

"Yes. It didn't take very long to get it where it belongs."

"Can you show me the warehouse?"

He shook his head. "Only Guardians and Agents are allowed in there."

Destiny wasn't surprised at his words, but she thought it would be worth asking. They both climbed back into the fancy golf cart, and Graham guided it back onto the main road of the complex. They passed what looked like a large dorm building. Graham told her that some of the agents lived there, if they wanted. He preferred to have his own place off the compound, but Trystan did rent one of the apartments.

There was a smaller apartment building next to the large one, and Graham told her that it was used for guests. Destiny assumed that she would be staying there. The next building had a shooting range inside. There were also many large rooms in which to learn and practice different types of self-defense. Throughout the entire complex and around each building were beautiful gardens and parks with large shade trees, benches and chairs to sit in, and picnic tables. Destiny was very impressed with the setup of the entire operation.

Graham stopped the cart in front of the last building, which was located northeast of headquarters, and Destiny looked at him curiously, waiting for an explanation.

"This is the cafeteria. We'll eat lunch here."

Destiny glanced at her smart watch she had put on just that morning and noticed that it was indeed lunch time, and her stomach growled hungrily, as she realized she hadn't eaten the protein bar Graham had given her that morning. Once they were inside, she realized that it was more than a basic cafeteria. There was a large restaurant which looked like it served more expensive meals. There were also many, smaller food establishments. The entire setup reminded Destiny of how food courts were at malls in her time.

Graham let her choose what they would eat. She noticed Mexican, deli sandwiches, hamburgers, and oriental foods, but she didn't recognize any of the names of the food establishments. She chose the sandwich restaurant. They ordered, and the food quickly was put in front of them.

Graham chose a table for them to sit, and Destiny noticed that he chose one that was well away from other people who were eating. Some of them greeted Graham or waved to him, but he just politely smiled. Once they were seated, Destiny waited until Graham started to eat his sandwich before asking the question she had wanted to ask all morning.

"Why was this agency started? It is obvious that this complex has been set up well. There is nothing like this in 2017. Or is there, and I just don't know about it?"

Graham set his sandwich down and looked at her for a long time, as if trying to make a decision. "This agency was started about five years ago. It wasn't around in your time. It was started out of necessity."

"What do you mean?"

Graham suddenly wanted to tell Destiny the history behind time travel. What would it hurt to tell her? She would be going back to her time soon, and she had already promised Jack she wouldn't tell anyone. Besides, like she had said to him, no one would believe her anyway.

He leaned back in his chair. "Do you remember the Y2K scare that happened in 1999?"

Destiny nodded, although she looked confused. Why was he asking her about that? "Yes, although I was still a child then. Everyone was worried because most of the computers were going to shut down, because they had only been made to run until December 31, 1999. When the date became January 1, 2000, everything that ran on computers was supposed to shut down, because it wouldn't recognize the date. A lot of people were worried about it. I do know a lot of people worked hard to keep the computers up and running."

Graham nodded.

"It always seemed silly to me. When January 1st came around and nothing happened, everyone calmed down and life went on."

"Well something did happen. The computers didn't fail, but something deep in the earth changed, and a certain power was released throughout the world, although no one was aware of it. Time-travel portals and devices started to work."

Destiny's eyes lit up. "Really? What kind of power?"

"We haven't been able to figure that out. Maybe it has to do with the magnetic field. Maybe it was some type of gas that was released. Who knows? But it did happen. At first time-travel devices were discovered by accident. Someone would find an old necklace, put it on and be transported to another place and time. Or someone would stand on a certain part of the earth and disappear, only to discover himself to be somewhere else.

"The people who discovered these devices kept quiet. Like what you expressed to Jack, who would believe them anyway? Some of them stayed where they traveled to; whether they were forced to or they chose to, we have no idea. Some devices only work certain times of the year. Others work only during certain times of the day. Many of them work all the time. Others only worked once, and then never worked again. Usually, as long as a person triggered the device properly, it works."

Destiny felt like she was listening to a fictional story. If she hadn't experienced time travel herself, she knew she wouldn't have given Graham's explanation a second thought. But it made sense to her, at least a little bit. After all, in 2017 novels, stories, and movies about time travel were becoming quite popular. Obviously, enough people were accidentally discovering time-travel devices, and maybe they told their stories through fiction.

"As the years passed, more and more people did believe in time travel. Some took advantage of it, wanting an adventure. Of course, they also started to fall into the wrong hands."

"What do you mean?"

"Some people discovered they could change history if they used the time travel devices in the right way."

"How? What could they change in history?"

"Start a war in a country, steal money, you think about it, they try to do it. Some changes that happened were only minor. Someone stays in the time they travel to, marry, and have a family. But minor can eventually become major.

For example, if someone were to travel back in time to buy a necklace and bring it back into the future, they sell it as a well-preserved antique, and make a lot of money off of it. Now, whoever was meant to have that necklace no longer gets it, and their descendants no longer have a family heirloom to sell when times get rough. That family no longer had the ability to make it, and some of them starve."

Destiny's eyes widened, and she didn't know what to say.

"That's only an example, but you can see how small actions snowball with time. The government decided we needed to put a stop to it. The *Time-Travel Guardians* was formed. I used to be a private investigator for *Shadow Works,* and I was quite good at it. They took the best of all of us, detectives, soldiers, PI's, and put us to work. Some of us investigate where the time-travel devices are and what year they are in. Once they find all the information, the agents go and collect them. They are stored in the warehouse for safe keeping."

"This is really interesting," Destiny said with a grin. She finished her sandwich and took a drink. "I bet you have the most interesting job in the world."

"It is fun, but it can be dangerous. Once we find a device, we try to remove it without anyone knowing what is going on. We'll purchase it with money from the owner's time or exchange it with something else. If the owner refuses to give it up, we will just take it. It is better to remove it from the owner than to allow it to become a device."

"So there weren't any time-travel devices before the year 2000?"

Graham shrugged his shoulders. "There might have been, but we don't know for sure. If there were, it wasn't common, and they weren't easy to find. Most likely, if there were devices, the person who triggered them never returned to their own time."

Destiny remembered something Graham had said at the beginning of the conversation. "You mentioned that there were also portals? What are those? How do they work?"

"Portals are places around the world. They aren't triggered by an object, but by something in the earth. All portals are found in very old places, areas that have been around for hundreds or thousands of years. Those are harder to find and harder to shut down, but Jack figured out a way to do it. They usually work spontaneously. Someone steps onto the area that has become a portal and instantly disappears. Some portals take people to places they weren't expecting. They have no idea what happened, how they got to the different time period, and they usually can't figure out how to return home. As far as how they work, again we have no idea."

"Wow, there is so much to take in." Destiny leaned back in her chair, thinking about everything she had just been told.

"There's more," Graham said with a smile.

Chapter Fourteen

Destiny looked at Graham warily, hoping Graham wasn't going to reiterate that he was sending her back to her time as soon as he could and that she didn't belong in his time.

"There are other changes that have happened since the year 2000, possibly even earlier. I've done a bit of research over the last few years. I started noticing that every child that has been born in the last twenty years or so is born with some type of gift."

Destiny frowned. "What do you mean, gifts?"

"Gifts like seeing visions, dreams, knowing what the future will hold, knowing what people are thinking or feeling, things like that."

Destiny's breath caught in her throat at Graham's words. There were other people in the world like her?

"I found out that at first the people who were born with these gifts didn't talk about it, or if they did tell someone, they were made fun of or others thought they were crazy. But since the year 2030, all children have been born with gifts. If they learn to use their gifts properly, it can help them throughout their lives. It is considered quite common for children to have them now, but it wasn't always that way."

"I know," Destiny said softly.

Graham looked at her carefully. "You know what?"

"I know about being born with a weird gift."

He kept looking at her. "Can you explain?" he finally asked, when she didn't say anything.

Destiny felt a familiar knot in her stomach, when the subject of her gift came up. She had been listening intently as Graham talked. She was in love with the man, but did she dare trust him with her gift?

"I was born with a gift," Graham said, as he took a bite of his sandwich. "I didn't recognize what it was though, until I was an adult."

"What...what is your gift?" Destiny asked, acknowledging for the first time that she wasn't the only weird person in the world.

"I'm an empath. I can feel other people's emotions, their feelings. When I touch someone, if I don't block it correctly, I can feel what they are feeling about whatever we are talking about."

Destiny sat back in her chair in silence. Graham was describing exactly what she felt when she touched someone, unless she blocked the emotions.

"I...think I am an empath, too," Destiny admitted softly.

Graham didn't say anything. He just watched her and listened, as she told him how she always knew she was weird, how her parents also thought something was wrong with her, about all the doctors and psychologists they took her to until she finally learned to hide it from everyone. She became good at pretending she was normal.

"You are normal, Destiny," Graham finally said. "You were born with an incredible gift. It's time to learn how to use it properly. I know in 2017, most people hide their gifts, but you don't have to do that here."

Another reason why I want to stay in your time, Destiny thought, but she didn't say it out loud.

"Think about what I said, and we can talk about it later, okay?"

Destiny nodded, glad that Graham had changed the subject. He started to talk about how he used to find people through the agency who had lost touch with their family members and other relatives.

Destiny was almost finished with her sandwich when a man approached them. He was almost as tall as Graham and had black hair and equally dark eyes. His hair was long and was tied back with a leather band. Even though she admitted to herself that this stranger was very good looking, she had an instant dislike for him, even before he spoke a word.

"Hi, Graham. I didn't know you were back," the man said as he came to a stop at their table.

Emotions flickered over Graham's face so quickly Destiny wondered if she had imagined them, but she wondered if he also disliked this man.

Graham stood and shook the man's hand. "Hello, Everett. I got back earlier this morning." Graham looked at Destiny. "Allow me to introduce Destiny Goodman. Destiny, this is Everett Harris. He is another agent that I work with."

Everett stuck his hand out, and Destiny and placed her hand in his. He bowed slightly, as he kissed the back of her hand, and her eyes widened at the gesture.

"It is an honor to meet such a lovely young woman," Everett said smoothly.

When Everett's lips touched her hand, Destiny immediately had an awful feeling in the pit of her stomach. She quickly pulled her hand away, as if she couldn't bear touching him. She wanted to wipe her hand on her skirt but refrained, knowing it would look like she was being rude.

"It's nice to meet you too," Destiny managed to say.

She had stayed seated through the entire exchange with Everett. Destiny received the distinct impression that Everett expected to be invited to join them, but Graham stayed on his feet, as they exchanged pleasantries. Destiny could tell the moment Everett received the unspoken message that he wasn't going to be included, when his eyes narrowed at Graham and then at Destiny. He finally told them to have a good day before leaving. Destiny sighed with relief as Graham sat back in his chair and continued to eat, as if the exchange hadn't bothered him.

Destiny had lost her appetite and sat back in her chair after pushing her plate away. She noticed her hands were shaking, and she was tempted to sit on them to stop the effect Everett had on her.

"I don't like him much either," Graham said nonchalantly, although he kept a careful eye on Destiny, as if making sure she was okay.

Destiny took a deep breath. "I had the most awful feeling when he touched me," she admitted.

"That's your gift talking to you," Graham said. "If you would allow it to surface instead of shoving it down deep inside you, it will help you, like it just did with Everett."

Destiny looked at Graham in amazement. She realized that he was right. Her gift of discernment had warned her that Everett wasn't a good man. It had never occurred to her that her gift could warn her of people like Everett. In fact, she suddenly realized that her gift seemed stronger than it had ever been before. She wasn't sure if it was because they had just talked about gifts in general, or if it was because she was at the moment living in the future, where almost everyone around her had some type of gift.

Graham broke the silence. "I have some things I need to wrap up from my job with Clara and her painting. How about I walk you to the apartment where you will be staying?"

Destiny hesitated before nodding in agreement, although she was reluctant to leave him. She was in a different world than she was used to, after all. She desperately wanted to stay in 2045, and she didn't want to give Graham a chance to suddenly decide it would be better off if he sent her back to her time.

She said little while Graham walked her to the guest apartments. When they arrived, he used a weird-looking key and opened one of the apartments, standing back until she went inside. He stayed at the entrance and bid her goodbye before closing the door and leaving.

Destiny felt a little let down. He had been acting so formal and hadn't lingered before saying goodbye. She looked at the closed door feeling deep regret. She started to turn away, but then the door suddenly opened again.

Leaving the door open, Graham strode toward her and pulled her into his arms. She wanted to laugh, but then his lips touched hers. All thoughts left as she enjoyed his kiss. Graham lit something inside her, and she was very glad she had followed him to his time. After a moment, Graham stepped back and grinned.

"I'll see you later," was all he said before shutting the door behind him again.

After he left, Destiny laughed out loud in the silence. She wanted to run after him and kiss him back. Then she suddenly realized that she was very tired, because the night before she had hardly had any sleep. It wouldn't hurt to rest for awhile.

Once she lay down on the comfortable bed in the only bedroom available in the apartment, it took some time for her mind to calm down. So much had happened to her in such a small amount of time. She thought again of how she wanted to stay in this time. She would be accepted, along with her gift. People wouldn't look at her as if she were weird or had something wrong with her. She knew that Graham would be able to help her understand her empathy and how to use it appropriately.

She wondered if anyone would actually miss her if she stayed. She had a few friends from college, but she considered them more like acquaintances. They got together a few times a month, but if one of them had other plans, no one seemed to miss them. Her boss, Aurora, would probably wonder what happened to her. She knew she would need to somehow let her know she was okay, so she didn't call the police and report her missing. It would be months before she heard from her parents, since they were so busy with their doctor jobs. She didn't need to worry about their missing her, at least not until Christmas for the annual Holiday dinner. Eventually, she was able to fall asleep. She ended up sleeping the rest of the day and through the night, missing the fact that Graham checked on her a few times, just to make sure she was okay.

Chapter Fifteen

The next morning, Destiny woke up to a pounding on her door. She glanced at her watch and realized it was almost nine o'clock, and she jumped out of bed in shock. She had never slept so late before. In fact, she had never slept so much at one time before. Evidently time travel could be tiring. The pounding started up again, and she heard the muffled voice of Graham.

"Destiny? Are you in there? Open the door, or I will open it myself. Destiny?"

She half ran to the front door before she realized she only had her underwear on, having slept in them because she didn't have any pajamas to wear.

"Just a minute!" she called. "I'll be there in a moment."

She ran back to her room and quickly pulled on her skirt and shirt she had worn the day before. She felt dingy in them and wondered if she could talk Graham into taking her shopping for some clothes. She had money in a national bank and wondered if those funds would still be good in this time. Hopefully that particular bank was still around. While she quickly dressed, she wondered why Graham hadn't just used the key he had had access to the day before.

As soon as she did up the last button on her shirt, she opened the door breathlessly.

"Hi," she greeted Graham with a wry grin. "I didn't mean to sleep so long."

Graham smiled back as he stepped inside. "I was getting worried. I was knocking for quite awhile."

"I guess I was tired," she admitted.

"I came to tell you that since I took the day off from work, it would be fun to show you around the city."

"I would love that."

Graham grinned. "Great." He looked at her for a moment. "Why don't I come back and get you in about an hour?"

Destiny was relieved that he was going to give her some time to clean up.

"That sounds like a plan. Should I go to the cafeteria for breakfast? Or is it too late for breakfast?"

"There should be some food in the kitchenette. I'm pretty sure there is coffee, cereal, fruit, and bread. But if you want to eat at the cafeteria, I can take you over there."

Destiny shook her head. "I'll just eat here."

After Graham left, Destiny went into the bathroom to take a shower. She had been too tired the night before to explore the small apartment, but now she spent a few minutes looking around. She could immediately tell that she was no longer in 2017. Things didn't look very different than from her time, but everything looked more modern. Instead of faucets to turn on the water, everything was computerized through touch screens. She figured out how the system worked pretty quickly though. There were buttons for cold and hot water, but there was also a button where she could punch in the temperature she wanted. After she did so, the water started to flow, and she touched it. It was already the perfect temperature. She pushed another button to start the shower. She opened a cupboard and found several large fluffy towels, different types of soaps, and hair supplies.

Once she was in the shower, she saw a panel where she could choose different sprays and steam. Deciding she didn't have time to play around with it, she left the settings as they were and took a shower. Twenty minutes later, she was again dressed and had braided her long blonde hair so it hung down her back.

"I'm going to insist that Graham take me to a clothing store," she said out loud. She hated the fact that she was wearing the same clothing she had worn when she had arrived with Graham the day before. When she put her smart watch back on, she realized it was going to run out of battery soon, and she had no way to charge it. She turned it off to save the battery, along with her phone since neither would work properly in this time anyway.

In the kitchen, she found that everything was also computerized. There was a large panel on one of the walls that seemed to control and program everything in the kitchen: the fridge, stove, and microwave which wasn't really a microwave like what she had in her own apartment but was more like a very fast-cooking oven. Again, she was able to get hot water the exact temperature that she wanted for some instant oatmeal she had found in the small pantry.

The coffee maker was also computerized and very quickly she had a cup in front of her. Breakfast was just like she enjoyed, a bowl of oatmeal with brown sugar sprinkled on it and a nicely toasted piece of whole-grain bread.

"I could get used to living in this time," she said with a smile.

She was ready and waiting for Graham when he knocked a second time that morning. When she opened it, her eyes took him in. His brown hair looked a bit unkept, as if he had just run his hands through it. He wore a pair of jeans, that looked similar to the ones worn in her time, along with a green shirt. She wanted to greet him with a kiss, but instead she stepped back and let him in.

Graham also looked her up and down appreciatively. "I can see you figured out how to use the apartment's computer system."

"Yep. It was quite fun actually to see how much things have changed less than thirty years from my time."

"Did you get some breakfast?"

"Yes." She waved her hand around the small, living room with its computerized entertainment center located on the far wall, with a strange looking bookshelf next to it. "I'll have to figure out how that works later. I'd love to watch a movie from your time."

"We can plan on doing that tonight."

"What are your plans for us today?" Destiny asked curiously.

"We can just drive around at first. I thought it would be fun to take you to the shopping mall for lunch."

"I assume the shopping mall would have some clothing?"

Graham looked at her curiously. "Of course. Why do you ask?"

"I really would like to get some new clothes to wear. I was wearing these yesterday. Plus, they look really old-fashioned in this time period."

Graham looked a little embarrassed. "That will be fine. I'm sorry I didn't even think about your clothing issue. Of course you'd want clean clothing to wear, and clothes that won't make you look like you came from the era before the war."

When Graham mentioned the war, Destiny made a note to herself to ask him about it later. She was very curious as to how it had started and what had happened.

"I have money in a major national bank," she said as she named a very well-known bank in her time. "Do you think I can use that money to purchase what I need?"

Graham shook his head. "Everything changed after the war, Destiny, including names for well-known banks and companies. There was a huge economic collapse that was caused by the war, and pretty much everyone lost all their money. It became worthless, except gold and silver. The dollar bills and coins people had before the war aren't worth anything now."

"Oh," Destiny said, her mind reeling with this information.

"But don't worry about it. I will pay for what you need."

Destiny hated the thought that she wouldn't be able to pay for the things she needed, but she decided to let him help her, and she'd figure out a way to pay him back later.

"Let's go," Graham said, as he opened the door.

Destiny followed him outside and to a waiting car. It was a different one than the one she had ridden in the day before. It looked like a very fancy sports car in her time. Graham opened the door for her, and she slid inside. When he was settled in his own seat, what would be the driver's side in her time, she watched as he voice-activated the car. She felt a slight vibration, but she didn't hear anything.

Graham touched a computer panel on the dashboard of the car and quickly punched in where he wanted to go. Then the car started to move. She really wanted to know how the vehicles ran, because it was obvious they weren't using gasoline. She decided to ask her questions later. Right now, she wanted to focus on her surroundings.

Graham directed the car to drive down the main street of Denver. It looked nothing like it was in her time, and she wondered why things were so different. She knew there would be some changes. After all, it was almost thirty years in the future, but nothing was the same. She finally mentioned it to Graham, not really expecting an answer.

When Graham didn't respond, she looked at him curiously. "I'm assuming you probably know why everything is so different," she said nonchalantly, trying to sound like she didn't really care one way or the other if he answered. She turned away from him and continued to look out the window at the different buildings, stores, and shops.

Graham cleared his throat. "There is a reason why things are so different, but I don't think it would be a good idea to tell you why. There are some things you really don't need to know right now, in your time of 2017."

"I'm going to guess. You're talking about the war you mentioned this morning, the one that hasn't happened yet in my time. There was a lot of destruction, death, and horror. I'm assuming America won the war, but there were a lot of changes and rebuilding that needed to be done in the aftermath."

Graham sighed. "We call it *The Terrible War*," he murmured.

Destiny reached out and took his hand. "I'm sorry. You lost a lot in that war, didn't you?"

He nodded. "Most of my family. Many friends. Only Trystan and I are left."

Tears formed in her eyes. "I'm so sorry," she said again.

"Everyone lost someone. I'm not going to tell you any more details – when it happened, the countries involved, or how it ended, so don't bother asking. But there is no reason to hide that it did happen. America won. We are still recovering from it, but life is good."

Something in Graham's voice told her he was through talking about this part of his past, and she decided to not push, although she was very curious about the details. She suddenly noticed that they were driving slowly down the street where the *Majestic Art Gallery* was located in her time period, and she was pleased to see that it was actually still there. The building was new, and there were other stores around it that were different, but it was still there.

"The gallery is still there!" she exclaimed with disbelief. It was the last thing she expected to see considering all of the changes there were with the rest of the city.

Graham grinned at her. "I wanted you to see it. There are some things that stay the same, no matter what happens."

"Can we stop and go inside?" she asked excitedly. "I'd love to see what it looks like now."

Graham hesitated before shaking his head. "Maybe another time."

Destiny wanted to insist he stop, but she also knew she needed to be glad he at least had shown her the gallery. "Where are we going now?" she asked as the car turned down a street and started to drive them away from the heart of Denver.

"We'll go to the shopping mall and get you some clothes. We can eat lunch there."

Destiny grinned at him, wanting to laugh out loud. She was having the time of her life. She knew that once she was back in her own time, she would want to have good memories of this impromptu trip to the future. She knew she would never be able to tell anyone what she had experienced, but she could have her memories. When they arrived at the mall, the car pulled into an empty parking lot without Graham giving it directions, and she wanted to know how it knew where to go, but she kept her questions to herself.

They walked inside, and she did her best to keep her mouth from hanging open in amazement. She didn't want to look like she was a person who had never seen a shopping mall in 2045 before, even though that was the case. The next few hours sped by. Graham guided her into a store where she was able to find everything she needed. She was glad people still wore jeans, although the fabric was a bit different than what she was used to. It was softer, and the color looked different. Graham told her the fabric would never fade. Graham encouraged her to purchase two pairs of jeans, along with four shirts, and something to sleep in. When it came to underclothing, Graham led her to the section, and then muttered under his breath that he'd be back, turned around and left. Destiny had to laugh before she quickly found what she needed, and she was glad to see that things hadn't changed much in way of design for women's underwear and bras. After she found a package of socks, Graham materialized beside her.

After purchasing her clothing, Graham took her to lunch, and she enjoyed some Mexican food. The enchiladas, tacos, refried beans, salsa tasted exactly what she was used to in her time, and she was glad to know that some things stayed the same. While they ate, Destiny brought up a subject that she had been pondering ever since she had met his boss, Jack M cGee.

"I enjoyed meeting your boss," Destiny said as she ate a chip after smothering it with salsa.

Graham glanced at her. "I have to admit, I expected him to not be very happy to discover that you had hitched a ride."

"I've been wondering if there is a connection between your boss and Clara."

He sat back and looked at her intently. When Destiny didn't say anything else, he waved a hand at her. "Go on. I'm sure you have a reason for saying that."

"Clara described Marcus to us, remember? She also described the odd clothing he wore. Mr. McGee seemed to match her description. He also seemed very interested in Clara's painting and in Clara herself, especially when we mentioned she had been married for a brief time before Marcus disappeared, and then she had had a daughter."

Graham shrugged, but Destiny could tell that he was listening. "Jack knows a lot of people. The ones he doesn't know, he is still aware of them. I suspect he has used time travel quite a bit. But I have to admit, I've been thinking the same. I'm not even sure he is really from 2045."

"What do you mean?"

"I just wonder if he was born long ago, like maybe the early 1900s, or even Clara's time. He somehow figured out how to travel to the future and decided to stay in my time."

"Or maybe he was forced to," Destiny suggested. "I wish we could ask him about his past."

Graham grinned. "Jack is a very knowledgeable man. He'll talk to you about any subject you want, except his family, where he is from, where he was born."

"Don't you find that interesting?" Destiny asked.

"Sure, but I greatly respect him. He had a huge hand in helping us recover from the war. When I first met him, he gave Trystan and me detective jobs without even an interview. He trained us and taught us everything he knew. He was the one who discovered about the threat of time-travel devices. Trystan and I were some of the first he hired to be Guardians for the new company. If he doesn't want to talk about his past, I figure that's his business.

I'm assuming you want me to ask him about any connection he might have with Clara. My feelings are that unless he voluntarily discloses the information, I will not bring it up."

Destiny nodded, knowing she needed to respect Graham's wish to leave things as they are, but she still felt strongly that somehow Jack McGee was Clara's Marcus.

Chapter Sixteen

When they were done with lunch and back in the car, they drove around for another hour until Destiny realized they were heading back to the *Shadow Work's* compound.

"Do you still want to see the gallery?" Graham asked.

"Of course," Destiny said firmly. "I'd love to see it."

"Very well then," he said as the car slid easily into a parking space between two other cars. "Just realized that anything is possible when it comes to time travel."

Destiny looked at him in confusion, but then she quickly forgot his words as she got out of the car. He was right behind her, as she opened the door and smiled in delight. The store was larger than it was in her time. It had a new, fresh smell to it, but the displays were set up almost the same way, although the content that was being sold was different. Paintings of landscapes and portraits hung on the walls. Pottery and ceramics were displayed on shelves. There was a case that offered different types of handmade jewelry; necklaces, rings, and bracelets.

"Hello, may I help you?" Destiny heard behind her. She didn't say anything, as she studied one of the paintings on the wall, but when she realized Graham hadn't answered, she turned around and gasped.

Standing in front of her was a woman that looked exactly like Aurora. But how could that be? Aurora lived in her time, and she knew she'd be at least in her 90s in 2045, or maybe even not alive.

Maybe she is Aurora's descendant, she thought.

"Hello, Destiny," Aurora's look-a-like said with a smile.

"How... how... You look like someone I know," Destiny stammered. "How do you know my name?"

"This is Aurora," Graham said with a grin.

"What? I don't understand. How did you get here?"

Aurora smiled in understanding. "I'm from this time. My family has operated and owned this gallery for a long time, since early 1900s actually. When the owner in your time died, and no one wanted to keep operating it, I received permission to run both stores. It needed to stay in operation."

"Really?" Destiny asked in disbelief. She was starting to wonder if time travel was even more common than she had even thought.

"Yes. I actually hired you with the idea that I would train you to someday take over the running of the shop in 2017, but I found I enjoyed going back and forth too much."

Destiny was so shocked, she couldn't speak. She glanced at Graham, and he grinned lazily at her, like he was saying, "What are you going to do about this?"

The gallery's door opened, and a group of ladies walked in. Aurora glanced at them.

"I need to help them. Feel free to look around as long as you want. Maybe later we can talk."

Destiny couldn't bring herself to move as Aurora glided away. She didn't know what to think. It was obvious that Graham knew that Aurora ran both stores in both time-periods. Why didn't he tell her that to begin with, when he showed up to collect Clara's painting the second time?

Emotions bubbled inside her that she didn't understand, but she did know that she couldn't stay in the gallery another moment. She turned and ran out of the store and continued to run down the street. She heard Graham call after her, but she didn't answer as she continued to run. She didn't know where she was going. She only knew she needed to get away from... everything. As she ran, she dodged people who were walking leisurely along the sidewalk. When she saw that the sidewalk ended as she came to an intersection, she turned down another street and kept running, knowing she had no way to cross safely. How in the world did people cross streets when the street lights didn't work properly? She heard footsteps behind her and instinctively knew that Graham was running after her, but she didn't stop. Tears started to run down her face as she ran, and she had to keep wiping them away, so she could see where she was going.

She saw what looked like a park in the distance and started to run towards it, but she started to slow down. She wasn't used to running so hard; she was starting to run out of breath, and her side hurt. She looked over her shoulder and could see Graham jogging about twenty feet behind her. She knew Graham could have caught up to her easily, but he seemed to be willing to let her run without catching up to her.

When she entered the park, she headed towards a bench under some shade trees and sat down, breathing heavily. A few minutes later, Graham sat down next to her without saying anything. They sat in silence for a long time, while Destiny caught her breath, tears still streaming down her cheeks.

"I'm sorry I ran off," she finally muttered, embarrassed that she had reacted like she had.

"I'm sorry I didn't prepare you that Aurora would be in the gallery," Graham said with regret. "I thought it would be a nice surprise. And you will figure it out soon enough when you return to your time."

"What is Aurora's role in all of this?" she asked, turning to look at him square in the eyes, letting him know she wasn't going to accept the excuse that he couldn't tell her because it might change history. She already knew too much.

Graham sighed and looked off into the distance. "She finds and recovers time-travel devices in your time. When she finds one, she lets Jack know where it is. Sometimes she purchases it for us and then holds it until we can go get it. That's what she did with Clara's painting; she purchased it from a man who used to own it in New York."

"If she is from your time, why not just bring it with her when she visits here?"

"The devices need to be recovered by a Time-Travel Guardian. It wouldn't be safe for her to bring it with her."

"But you acted like you didn't know her. You also bought that painting from her. I saw the entire transaction," Destiny said angrily.

"That's because she did purchase it. I needed to reimburse her."

Destiny nodded. It made sense to her in a weird sort of way. She sighed and leaned her head back against the bench. She was so tired.

Graham watched Destiny rest her head against the bench. It was all he could do to not gather her into his arms. Her reaction to seeing Aurora surprised him. She had shown so much excitement, as she had experienced his time over the last few days. He knew he had handled things badly. He didn't know what he had expected her to do when she found out about Aurora, but he didn't expect her to run off like she had.

He breathed out a frustrated breath and then did what he wanted to do. He put his arms around her. Destiny allowed him to hold her, and she leaned her head against his chest. For a long while they sat that way. He touched her face and then let his hand run through some of the strands that had come lose from the braid while she had been running. Then he tipped her face and did what he had been trying to avoid the entire day. He bent and kissed her.

Kissing Destiny was something he hadn't ever experienced with anyone else. He didn't know what the future was going to entail for the two of them, but he knew he was never going to be the same again. He would never feel for anyone else what he felt for her.

When he finally stopped the kiss, he kept her close to him. Neither of them talked. After awhile, Destiny started to move, and he knew it was time to go. They both silently stood and walked slowly to the car. He kept her hand in his the entire time. The feelings, the emotions were so strong between them, and he knew Destiny was very aware of what was developing between the two of them.

The next day, Destiny found herself with Graham in the cafeteria eating breakfast. When he had come to collect her that morning, she tried to act like everything was fine. But ever since Graham had dropped her off at the guest apartment the night before, she had been thinking. She had spent most of the night thinking. Around three o'clock she had finally made a decision. She knew what she wanted to do, what she needed to do. Once she made her decision, she felt a great peace come over her, and she was able to sleep deeply until just before Graham showed up to take her to breakfast.

When she saw him, her heart flooded with the peace she felt in the middle of the night, again confirming that her decision was the right one.

Now, she hoped he would understand.

While they ate, Graham kept up the conversation. He told her he was willing to do whatever she wanted, since he still had some time off and gave suggestions as to what they could do or see. Destiny didn't give him any hint of what she wanted to do until she ate her last bite of eggs and finished her coffee.

"I want to talk to your boss," she announced.

"What?" Graham asked, alarm in his eyes.

Destiny knew that he was feeling nervous at her behavior that morning. She knew he could feel something had changed; he just didn't know what.

"I want to talk to Jack," she repeated.

Graham pushed his plate away and leaned back in his chair, his arms folded against his chest. "Can I ask what about?"

"Sure," Destiny said agreeably. She tried to sound like she didn't care what Graham thought about her decision, but deep down she cared very much. She wasn't sure what his reaction was going to be.

When Destiny didn't say anything more, he said, "Care to clue me in?"

"I am going to ask Jack if I can stay here, in your time, in 2045," she said, making sure that Graham knew exactly what she was asking.

Graham didn't say anything, and Destiny did her best to not squirm under his intense gaze.

"Why?" he finally asked.

"Lots of reasons."

"Care to clue me in?" he asked again when she didn't elaborate.

"I like it here. I have to admit that you are right. I know too much to go back to my time. It would be difficult living there with all that I know about the future. Plus the information about this 'war' you won't tell me about. I would be living on pins and needles all the time, wondering when it was going to start. All I know is that it's going to be terrible. Well, I don't want to live through it, if I do happen to live through it."

She stopped talking to see what Graham's reaction was, but she couldn't tell. He was looking at her as she talked, but she couldn't tell if he was happy about her decision or not. She decided to keep going.

"Aurora said she hired me to eventually take over running the *Majestic Art Gallery*. I figure I can work here as well as in 2017. I'm sure there are some things that are different, but I'm a fast learner. I will be able to support myself."

She stopped again and looked at him, her eyes softening as she prepared herself for whatever his reaction would be to her next words.

"And I have discovered that I love you. If I don't stay, I will end up having a life like Clara did. I would never be able to love someone else."

For a few seconds, Graham didn't react to her words, but then he did something that forever linked them together. He slowly took her hand in his, stood, and pulled her to her feet. He put his arms around her and just held her. There, in the middle of a busy cafeteria o f *Shadow Works*. Destiny sighed with relief and hugged him back. Feelings flew through both of them, and they communicated without words. Destiny knew that Graham loved her too.

"Let's get out of here," Graham muttered, as he realized they had captured quite a few of his coworkers' attention. He took her hand and practically dragged her out of the cafeteria. She followed him, as he found an empty picnic table in the compound's vast park.

"I love you, Destiny Goodman," Graham said, after they sat next to each other. "I realized that last night, but after how upset you were when you saw Aurora, I thought I had totally messed things up between us."

"I admit I was upset, but not for the reasons you think," Destiny admitted. "I think a lot of it was I have experienced a lot of... different, new, strange things, since I literally ran into you outside that cafe. I think my emotions were catching up to me. I also realized I wanted to stay here, but I didn't think you would want me to."

"I definitely want you to stay. I am a bit concerned about changing history, yours and mine, but I also think those things will work out."

"I have some thoughts about what you told me, how something in the earth triggered time-travel devices all over the world around the year 2000. I don't think whatever caused them to activate was an accident. Things like that don't happen just by chance."

"Maybe so," Graham agreed carefully.

"I also think we were meant to meet. There is something between us that is too strong, too powerful to ignore. This type of love can't happen by chance. It's meant to be."

Graham continued to look at her. He then took her hand in his, and she knew he was reading her, and she was doing the same with him. For the first time, she allowed her gift to be used to its full extent. Respect, simplicity, happiness, power, and pure love flowed between them. Even though they weren't married and hadn't yet shared a bed, a bond had formed between them that could never be broken.

Keeping her hand in his, Graham stood. "Come. Let's go talk to Jack."

Chapter Seventeen

G raham and Destiny quickly walked to the large building where Jack's office was. As they walked, Graham grew more and more excited. He couldn't believe what was happening. He had finally found the woman he wanted to spend the rest of his life with, and he didn't want to let her go. He only hoped Jack was going to agree that Destiny could stay. But he knew what he was going to do if he didn't.

All too soon the two of them were standing in Jack's office in front of his secretary. After Graham informed her that they wanted to talk to Jack, his heart dropped when the secretary scanned the schedule that was in front of her.

"Jack has meetings all day, and I can't fit you in. You'll need to make an appointment."

Graham opened his mouth, ready to argue, when Jack's door opened.

"Let them in, Gladys, and reschedule the next appointment to later today or tomorrow. I'll stay late tonight if I need to."

Graham sighed with relief. He didn't know if either he or Destiny could have waited another day.

"Sit down, sit down," Jack said, as Graham entered his office, Destiny's hand still tucked in his. "What can I do for you two?"

Destiny immediately spoke up. "I have decided I don't want to go back to my time, to 2017. I want to stay here."

"Is that so?" Jack asked with a small smile on his face. "And why do you want to stay here? Besides the obvious, of course, the advanced technology, our beautiful city."

Destiny waved her other hand in the air. "I have to admit, I find all the changes interesting, but I don't want to stay because of that. I want to stay with Graham."

"Are you asking my permission, young lady?" Jack asked.

Destiny hesitated before nodding, and Graham knew she didn't want his permission. She wanted to insist she stay no matter what.

"We both know that things would be much easier on all of us if you agree to it," Graham spoke up. "But if you don't, I am prepared to go back with her and live in her time."

Jack's eyes narrowed. "You'd give up your job here and all that you have, for her?"

Graham nodded. "I love her, sir."

"And what about Trystan?"

Graham didn't say anything. He knew it would be difficult to leave his brother behind, but he figured he'd do something about that if he had to.

"I see, I see," Jack murmured, as he stood and walked to the large window behind his desk and looked out of it for a moment.

Destiny looked at him with confusion in her eyes, and Graham squeezed her hand in assurance. They would deal with whatever Jack decided, together.

Finally Jack turned away from the window. "Have you downloaded the information about your last trip to the computer?"

"No, sir. My watch stopped working, remember?"

"Try it again."

Graham let go of Destiny's hand long enough to push a few buttons. He looked up in surprise.

"It seems to be working now."

"Let's see what went on during the time you were gone."

After a few seconds of pushing a few buttons, Graham nodded. "It's downloaded, sir."

"Good, good," Jack said, as he touched some keys on his computer and started to read. All was quiet in the large office, and Graham had to resist the urge to stand up and pace. So much was riding on the next few minutes.

"Interesting, interesting," Jack muttered to himself, as he finished reading and leaned back in his chair.

"Can I say something before you make your decision?" Destiny asked.

"Of course, young lady," Jack said with a twinkle in his eyes.

"I just wanted to let you know that the love I feel for Graham is much like the love Clara had for Marcus."

Jack's eyes narrowed, as he looked at her silently.

"Clara was never able to love another man. I know deep in my heart that it would be the same for me," Destiny continued.

Graham knew that Destiny was trying, in her own way, to let Jack know that she suspected a connection between his boss and Clara.

Jack nodded slightly and then looked at Graham. "I assume you took Destiny to the gallery?"

Graham grinned. With those words, he knew Jack was going to agree to their plan. "Yes. She knows about Aurora."

"I thought I could work there," Destiny spoke up.

"Well, after what you both have told me, and after reading the report you downloaded, Graham, I will approve your request to stay here."

"Oh, thank you," Destiny breathed. Tears flowed down her face.

"There are rules that you both will need to agree to, of course. Graham, you may take Destiny back to 2017 to collect any of her belongings she needs. Destiny, you cannot tell anyone where you are going. Will there be family or friends who will miss you?"

"I have a few friends, but they are more like acquaintances. I can just tell them I'm moving to another city, and they won't think anything of it. I do have my parents, but we don't keep in touch with each other very often. I don't know if they will care or not if they don't hear from me."

"I will take care of your parents," Jack said. "The third rule is that neither of you will tell anyone in Destiny's time or this one where she is from. Graham, it is your job to educate her and make sure she fits in as well as possible."

"Okay," Graham agreed.

"And... the last rule. If things do not work out between you, if you both decide not to further your relationship, Destiny, you need to understand that there is no going back. You will need to stay in this time until your death."

"I understand," Destiny said with a smile.

"It is done then," Jack said, as he stood to his feet, after pounding his hands on the desk.

Graham and Destiny did the same.

"Thank you, sir," Destiny said, happiness shining in her eyes.

"You're welcome, young lady. I think you will be a great asset to this time period. I will talk to Aurora and make arrangements for you to start working there as soon as you are ready. You may also stay in the guest apartment you are in as long as you need to."

"Thank you," Destiny said again, relief in her voice.

"Graham, plan on taking whatever days you need to get Destiny settled. Let me know when you are ready for a new job."

"Yes, sir."

Graham and Destiny walked to the door, but Jack stopped them before they opened it. "And Destiny, it looks like I might need to do something about Clara, don't I."

Destiny didn't say anything, but she looked at him with compassion in her eyes. Graham opened the door, and they quickly walked past Gladys and to the elevators. Once they were inside, Destiny stepped into his arms.

"I'm so glad he understood, and he agreed," she said.

Graham kissed the top of her head. "So am I. But I sure would like to see what he was reading from the information from my watch."

Destiny grinned. "I'd like to know what he's going to do about Clara."

The next few days passed in a blur for Destiny. Now that Graham's watch was back in working mode, he took her back to 2017, landing in her apartment. She took her time going through her things, but she really didn't have much. Most of her clothes wouldn't work for Graham's time period, so she left most of them hanging in her closet. She ended up packing one suitcase with her belongings. Most of what she brought were some journals she had written in when she was younger, along with a photo album, some of her favorite books including the one Clara had given her. At the last minute she included her tablet, along with the chargers for her phone and smart watch even though she knew they most likely wouldn't work in 2045. They each had information on them that she wasn't willing to lose, along with her library of eBooks and favorite movies. Graham told her that they would be able to transfer the files from them to a new tablet and phone, even though hers were considered "ancient" in 2045.

"They're considered antiques, my dear," Graham said with a grin.

When she was ready, Graham's watch took them back to his apartment. Because Destiny had time traveled twice in one day, she was exhausted and promptly fell asleep on Graham's couch.

Graham had gone into his kitchen to prepare a meal. Destiny missed it when he set the food he had prepared on the coffee table and brushed back her hair from her face.

"It seems like time travel is hard on you," he murmured. "It's a good thing this was our last trip."

Destiny ended up sleeping through the night and woke the next day to delicious smells. She stretched and then sat up, pushing a blanket away that Graham had obviously used to cover her the night before. Her eyes widened at the large aquarium that was tucked in the corner, and she got up to look at it. She couldn't remember seeing it when she first came to Graham's apartment, but then everything was so new to her. She had only noticed the differences between her time and Graham's.

"But now his time is my time," she murmured to herself.

"Oh, looks like sleeping beauty is awake," Graham said, as he entered the room.

Destiny smiled at him.

"I was wondering if I was going to have to kiss you awake," he continued.

"I think your cooking did the job, but you can kiss me anyway," Destiny said, as she walked into his arms.

Chapter Eighteen

Over the next few months, Destiny settled into her new life. With Jack's support, Graham took some time off to help her acclimatize living in 2045. Destiny loved learning about her new world, but it was also exhausting. By the end of each day, she would feel so tired, she fell asleep almost before her head hit the pillow. But she woke up each morning rested and ready to experience more of what Graham wanted to teach her. She couldn't help but constantly compare her new world to the old. Technology was greatly more advanced than in her time. It seemed as if almost everything ran by computers, and this was probably the hardest part of 2045 that she had to learn. In her time, she used computers daily, but she only had known the basics. As Graham taught her how to run the new systems, she realized that it wasn't going to be easy to learn everything in a short amount of time. One of the first things Graham reminded her of was that no one could know what time period she was actually from, except for a few select people.

Graham was willing to talk to her and show her whatever she had interest in, except one subject, and that was the war. The few times Destiny brought it up, Graham would either change the subject or walk away. Destiny soon realized that whatever happened during that war, it had deeply scarred Graham in some way. She also learned that almost everyone else also avoided the subject. Even though it had been almost twenty years ago, it had obviously changed how people saw and lived their lives. Destiny knew that she could easily have gone to the local library or even searched on the computers about the war and could have learned all that she wanted to know, but for some reason she hesitated. Did she really want to know about something that would have been in her near future if she had stayed in her time? She decided that she wasn't ready for the truth.

After she had been in 2045 for about a month, she started to work in the gallery with Aurora. Her boss seemed very happy to have her around. After a few weeks of intense training on how to operate the computer system, Aurora left for 2017 to hire someone else to help run that store. It had been closed since Destiny had left, and Aurora was anxious to open the gallery again. She knew that Aurora would be checking up on her periodically but would be spending most of her time in 2017. Destiny was nervous about being left on her own after Aurora left, but she soon learned that one of the things about the computer system in 2045, it almost always worked perfectly. Whenever she had questions or needed help for anything, all she had to do was "ask" the computer for help, and instantly the issue was fixed or the question answered.

Once she started working in the gallery, Graham started to also go back to work with the agency. They spent each evening together, which became Destiny's favorite time of her days. Graham had requested that he work as a regular detective for awhile, so he could continue to help Destiny.

There was only one thing that Destiny had a hard time with. Ever since they had returned from her time with her belongings, Graham hadn't kissed her. At first, she decided it was because they were so busy, and he still would hold her hand and always would give her wonderful hugs when they parted each night. But he never tried to kiss her again, since the day in Jack's office, and she missed them. It seemed as if he was waiting for something, but for what?

Graham sat back in his chair and sighed. It had been a long morning, and he was looking forward to seeing Destiny for lunch. When she first told him she wanted to stay in his time, he was ecstatic. Even though they had only been together for a few days, he had fallen for her fast. Once she was settled in the guest apartment in the compound, Graham had started "how to live in 2045" lessons. He enjoyed watching Destiny as she learned new things.

Now, almost three months later, Destiny seemed to be doing well and was spending her days at the gallery. Graham had felt that he needed to stick around for awhile and not accept any new time-travel jobs. Jack had been understanding, but he had urged Graham to let him know when he was ready, since more and more time-travel devices were being found almost daily. Graham had been content with helping people with their genealogy lines, but today he found what Jack would describe as a "hole." He knew that when he sent the information to Jack, his boss would flag it as what he called a possible time-travel break.

Graham stood up and walked to the window in his office and looked outside. He realized that now that Destiny was doing so well, he was starting to get antsy. He wanted to start accepting time-travel jobs again. He decided to let Jack know he was ready. Maybe he'd be willing to let Graham take over the information he had just found. Just then his computer buzzed, letting him know he had a call.

When Graham opened up the call, he saw it was Jack, and he smiled to himself. Now was as good as time as any to let Jack know of his decision.

"Hi, Jack," Graham greeted his boss. "What's up?"

"I just opened up the files you sent me. You are right. It does look like a time breach. How would you like to take this job?"

"I was just thinking about that," Graham admitted. "Destiny seems to be doing okay. I think it will be alright to start being a Guardian again."

"Good, good," Jack said. "I'll do a bit of research and get back with you."

After signing off, Graham sat back in his chair, but then he jumped up again. He knew that Jack would most likely have the information he would need by the end of the day. He decided he would go to the gallery and let Destiny know he most likely would be gone for a few days.

Once he was outside, he debated about using the company car he had at his disposal or walk to the gallery. Glancing at the clear blue sky, he decided to walk, even though it would take about half an hour to do so. He needed the exercise, and the sun felt good on his face since it was the first time in almost a week that they'd had a sunny day.

When he arrived at the gallery, he was relieved to see that Destiny was at the front counter reading something on the tablet he had given her, and the shop was empty at the moment. When he walked into the building, she looked up and smiled.

"Hi, Graham," she said, as she walked around the counter and greeted him with a hug. "What brings you here this time of day?"

"I have something I wanted to talk to you about," Graham explained.

"Really?" she asked. "Now is as good a time as any. For some reason, today has been quite slow, most likely because it's the first sunny day we've had for awhile. Everyone is probably out enjoying the good weather."

They both walked to a small area Aurora had created for people to relax and enjoy the atmosphere of the gallery. There were two small sofas that sat across from each other, with a coffee table in between them. Tucked in the corner was a small table with a coffee maker which always held fresh coffee, along with a plate of pastries from the bakery down the street.

"What do you want to tell me?" she asked curiously.

Graham waited until he filled two mugs with coffee before sitting beside her and handing her one. "I think you are doing well acclimatizing to this time period, don't you?"

"Sure," Destiny agreed. "I've had a few moments of panic, but for the most part, it's been pretty easy. I'm very grateful I have this job and a way to support myself."

"When I was working today, I was doing a family line for an old client of ours. I found a time breach, a hole in their genealogy."

Graham noticed that Destiny froze, as she brought her coffee mug to her lips. After a moment, she carefully set the mug on the table. He knew she was aware of what that meant.

"What are you trying to tell me, Graham?"

"Someone needs to take this job, Destiny," Graham said. "Jack agrees with me, and I think since you are doing so well, I should accept this job."

"Do you know where you would be going?"

"Not exactly. Jack is doing the final research now, but the hole in the family line is in the 1930s."

Destiny didn't reply, and, after a moment, Graham grew concerned. "Are you okay? I know you might be nervous that I'll be gone, but it should only be a few days at the most."

Destiny smiled at him, but he could tell it was forced. "Of course I'll be okay. I know I can contact Jack if I need help with anything, and, like you just said, it's only for a few days."

Graham narrowed his eyes at her, as he grew concerned. He could tell that she wasn't happy at all that he was planning on leaving. He opened his mouth to question her, but just then the door opened and a group of three ladies came in.

Destiny glanced at the group and stood. "I need to get back to work."

"Okay, I'll just wait here until they leave. We need to talk about this."

Destiny gave a short nod before turning to her customers. Graham watched her for a few minutes, trying to decide what was going on in her head. From what he could tell, she wasn't happy that he was going to start being a Guardian again. But why would she be upset? She knew that having him around all the time was only temporary. She was very aware of what his job entailed. After all, it was the reason why they met. Graham waited for almost an hour to talk to her, but she continued to stay busy with her customers. He finally gave her a wave and left. He needed to make sure his backpack was ready to go for this new job. While he was waiting, Jack had sent him the particulars of the job. He would be traveling to San Francisco in 1936. He was supposed to find an old pocket watch that had become a time-travel device. He couldn't stop what happened with the time breach, but he could stop it from happening again. He was to leave first thing in the morning.

Once he arrived at his own apartment, he sent a message to Destiny, asking her to come to his place when she was done working.

Destiny watched out the corner of her eye as Graham waved to her and then left the store. She was amazed at how busy the shop had become since most of the day had been very slow. She wanted to run after him and demand that they talk, but she knew she couldn't do that. Aurora was counting on her to be a professional. She needed to do her work, knowing that they could talk later. For the rest of the day, Destiny was busy with customers, but she couldn't get what Graham had told her out of her mind. She knew that Graham had chosen to not accept any time-travel jobs because of her, and she was very grateful that he was willing to stick around. But she was doing well now, and she knew there was no reason for Graham to continue turning down jobs. He was a Time-Travel Guardian, and she didn't want to stand in the way of his job. But when he told her that he was going on a job, her heart fell to the pit of her stomach. She was actually terrified that he was leaving, but she didn't understand why.

When six o'clock finally rolled around, Destiny escorted the last customer out the door and then locked it. She leaned back against the cool glass for a moment with her eyes shut. It had been so busy since Graham had left, Destiny almost couldn't handle all the customer's questions and purchases. This type of day had happened more and more often, and she had wondered if she should ask Aurora if she would be willing to hire another girl to help, at least in the afternoons. She knew that some of the people who had come in had left because they didn't get the help they needed.

"Oh, well," Destiny muttered to herself. She still had to finish the evening chores before she could go home. She quickly went through the list: transfer the money that was made to the electronic bank, sweep the floor, pour out the old coffee and get the machine ready to make a new pot in the morning, and straighten up each section of the gallery, restocking the areas she needed to. She hurried as quickly as she could, because she really wanted to talk to Graham before he left. He had sent her a message to come to his apartment when she was done, and she breathed a sigh of relief when she was finally on her way in the first, driverless car that she had owned.

Graham had actually made arrangements for her to have her own car, and she loved it. At first, she had a hard time letting the car do its job. She worried that the computer in the car would have some kind of glitch and would make a wrong turn or would even change lanes at the wrong time and would hit another car. The city had stop lights, but they ran differently than she was used to. They communicated with all the cars on the road and directed each car to stop, slow down or speed up accordingly, as they went through intersections. It actually was an efficient arrangement, but it was hard to get used to. She learned to sit on her hands as the car moved. Otherwise, she would be clutching the seat or side of the car every time she was afraid something wasn't working correctly. After three months in 2045, she could now admit that she trusted her car with her life.

When she arrived at Graham's apartment, she gave instructions for the car to park in her usual spot. Graham's apartment was on the second floor, and soon she was standing in front of his door, using her fingerprint to let herself into his rooms after giving the door a sharp knock. When she entered, the door closed softly behind her and automatically locked. She immediately had the sense that the apartment was empty.

"Graham?" she called, as she looked around the living room and then walked towards the kitchen. "Graham? I've come like you asked."

There was no answer. When she entered the kitchen, she saw a piece of paper on the table. Walking closer, she saw her name on it, and picked it up.

Destiny,

Jack was able to finish the research quickly and wanted me to get started on this case as soon as possible. I should be home in a few days. Feel free to stay at my apartment if you wish.

Can you feed my fish for me?

Love, Graham

Destiny dropped the letter in disbelief and sat down on a chair. It seemed like her life was changing again, and this time she didn't like it. Then she realized why she was so upset.

What if something happened to Graham, and he didn't return? What if he ended up stuck in whatever time period he had traveled to?

She sat for quite a while in Graham's kitchen, the room becoming dark as night fell, before she finally stood up and turned on the lights. She opened up the freezer and pulled out a reheatable meal, stuck it in the oven, and then went to feed Graham's fish. She ate her meal in front of Graham's large, screenless TV which took up almost half of the wall. She found a movie, but she had a hard time focusing it. Deep down she knew Graham most likely wasn't in danger. He had been a Time-Travel Guardian for years before she had met him. She knew there were standards set up for if Graham did get in a situation that he needed to get out of; he would be immediately removed and taken back to his time, but she didn't know what those standards were.

She finally fell asleep on Graham's comfortable sofa in the early morning hours. The next day when she walked into the gallery, Aurora was behind the counter working on some paperwork. Destiny was so glad to see her boss that she almost broke down in tears.

"Hello, dear," Aurora greeted her with a smile. "I see you have been having some busy days lately."

Destiny nodded, as she set her belongings behind the counter. "It has been quite busy. I've been thinking that it might be a good idea to hire another person, at least for the afternoons."

Aurora shook her head. "That won't be necessary. I will be staying in this time period from now on."

"Oh, really?" Destiny asked curiously. "So I guess the new lady you hired for the 2017 gallery is working out?"

"No, I'm afraid not. In fact, she accidentally left the back door unlocked a few days ago after she left for the night, and the gallery was robbed."

"Oh, no," Destiny breathed in disbelief.

"Whoever did it was probably looking for money. They didn't find any, because, as you know, we never keep money there overnight. So they took some of the more expensive items, but they trashed the rest. They even started a fire in the back room, but luckily the fire alarm went off and that scared them off. The fire was put out quickly by firemen but not soon enough to stop any damage. I do have insurance and will be using that to pay our suppliers for what they lost, but I will not be reopening the gallery."

"I'm so sorry, Aurora," she said, following her instincts to give the older woman a hug of comfort. Aurora accepted it, and for a moment she allowed the hug.

"What's done is done, I guess. To be honest, I've been feeling more and more unsafe and uncomfortable in 2017. I'd always planned to be gone before...." Aurora stopped talking and pretended to be busy with some paperwork in front of her.

"Before what? Are you talking about the war?" Destiny asked.

Aurora shrugged. "It's not my favorite subject."

Destiny wanted to ask more questions, but she decided to let it drop. "I'm really sorry about your shop, but I'm glad you are going to be here all the time."

Aurora looked at her sharply, as if suddenly realizing that Destiny was upset. "I get the feeling you are upset about something else."

"Yes," Destiny sighed. She knew Aurora was probably the only person she could talk to about her concerns regarding Graham being a Time-Travel Guardian. "Graham was sent out on a job. He left last night."

Aurora looked a little confused. "Well, my dear. That shouldn't be too surprising. After all, it was because of his job that you two even found each other."

"I know, but I can't get it out of my head that something could happen. What if he inadvertently gets into a situation that is dangerous, and he isn't able to come back?" Tears flooded her eyes as she spoke.

"Oh, my dear." This time it was Aurora comforting her. "Graham will be fine. In all my years helping recover devices, never once did I hear of an instance that a Time-Travel Guardian never returned."

"Really?" Destiny asked with a watery voice.

"Yes, really." Aurora squinted her eyes in concern. "Are you sure this is all it is? Are you sure you aren't worried about something else?"

Destiny shrugged, not sure what Aurora meant.

"You have had so many changes in your life. Maybe some of this is just residual emotion. You've done an excellent job learning all you have and trying to fit in here in this time, but I'm sure it's been stressful."

"I want to be here, Aurora," Destiny said firmly.

"I know you do, and Jack wouldn't have allowed it if he hadn't thought you could handle it."

Destiny glanced at the clock and saw that it was almost time to open. "The boxes for the Native-American display arrived yesterday just before closing. I'll go start stocking those shelves."

Aurora nodded her agreement. "That's fine dear. Oh, and Destiny, have you expressed any of these feelings to Graham?"

Destiny shook her head. "No, I guess I've been reluctant, because I don't want him to regret helping me stay here."

"Talk to him, my dear. You may be surprised."

Destiny shrugged her shoulders noncommittally. "I'll think about it."

As she opened the first box, she was glad she had talked to Aurora and that she was going to be staying in this time from now on. She felt awful about what had happened to her other store, but it would be good to have a woman close to her who understood what was going on.

Graham did get home late the next day. When he was back, he sent a message to Destiny. When Aurora found out, she encouraged her to go to him. As Destiny rode to his apartment, she was still having mixed feelings about talking to Graham. When she gave the door her usual knock before entering, she was so glad to see Graham that she ran into his arms.

"Oomph," Graham grunted, as Destiny threw her arms around him, and he gave her a hard kiss on her mouth. "I'm glad to see you, too."

Then Destiny embarrassed herself and started to cry.

"What's wrong?" Graham asked with concern.

"Oh," Destiny whispered, as she quickly wiped the tears away, although more still came. "I'm just glad your home."

After a few moments, Graham led her to his couch. "What's going on, Destiny? I felt like something was wrong when I last saw you."

"I'm sorry," Destiny said, as she used a handkerchief he produced from his pocket. "I don't know what's come over me."

Graham let her cry for a few minutes before taking her hand in his. "I have to ask, are you starting to have second thoughts about being in my time? Is that it?"

Destiny looked at him in shock. "No! I'm not having second thoughts, I promise."

"Then why all the tears?"

"I guess I just had a hard time with the idea that you had started working as a Time-Travel Guardian again," she admitted softly.

Graham's eyes narrowed. "I know I took some time off, but did you think I'd never go back?"

"Yes, no, I don't know," she said. "I guess I was just surprised. You hadn't said anything and.."

"And what?" Graham asked when she didn't finish.

"I am very worried that on one of your time travel jobs, something will happen and..."

"And I won't come back."

"Yes, you won't come back," she said softly.

Graham sighed. "I can't stop being a Guardian, Destiny."

"I know. I'm being illogical. I'm sure I'll get over it."

"Let me show you something about this watch. I'm going to show you how it works, okay?"

Destiny nodded, but she looked surprised. She remembered having asked him how it worked when she was by the ocean in Clara's time, but he had refused to answer her questions and had only given vague answers.

"It looks like an antique watch that people used to wear in the early 1900s."

"Jack designed it, and he made it look that way on purpose. But when I do this..." Graham pushed a button found underneath, and a new watch face appeared. "This screen is how I time travel. I give the watch all the information it needs – what era I'm traveling to, the exact location, what time of day, and date. I also insert a time frame. It will automatically bring me back here by that time, no matter what is going on wherever I'm at. When I'm ready to go back, if it's before that time period, I just push this button, and it takes me back. And see this black button?"

Destiny nodded.

"It's an SOS button. If I'm in trouble at all and can't operate my watch for any reason, this SOS button will alert Jack, and he will get me back. There is absolutely no reason for me to end up stuck in a time not of my choosing."

Destiny looked carefully at the band of the watch for the first time. "The band looks very different. It's almost like you can't take it off."

"I can't. I can't take the watch off even if I wanted to. It is essentially sealed on my wrist. And one other thing. I am the only one who can operate it. No one else can."

Destiny nodded her understanding. "I know that this is who you are, a Time-Travel Guardian. I guess I was just..."

"I know I didn't get to talk to you about leaving, and I apologize for that. Jack found out some information and wanted me to leave quickly, and it was a good thing I did."

"Can you tell me where you went?"

Graham shook his head. "The less you know about the jobs I go on, the better. I am only supposed to talk to other Guardians about the jobs."

Destiny nodded, expecting that answer. "I talked to Aurora today about all of this. She helped me see that I've had so many changes in my life over the last few months, I probably just reached my limit when you had to leave so quickly. I promise that I don't have a problem with your job. I understand that what you do is important."

"Aurora is right. You have had a lot of changes in your life. And I've been wanting to make one more, but maybe I should give you some more time."

"What is it?" Destiny asked curiously.

Graham looked into her eyes as if he was trying to decide something. Then he pushed her gently away. "Just a minute. I'll be back."

Destiny waited while Graham went into his bedroom and then quickly returned.

"I've been trying to decide if this is the best time, so if you need more time, I'm fine with that."

"What are you talking about?" Destiny asked. Then she looked down at Graham's hand and noticed he was holding a small, black box. Was he holding what she thought he was holding?

"Destiny Goodman, will you marry me?"

Destiny's eyes again filled with tears. "Oh, Graham, of course I'll marry you."

Graham sighed with relief, as she again threw herself into his arms.

"I love you, Destiny. I think the best thing that ever happened to me was when you ran into me that day outside that cafe."

"What?" Destiny laughed. "You ran into me!"

Graham laughed with her. "How ever it happened, I'm glad it did."

"I love you too, Graham. I will be honored to be your wife."

Then Graham cupped her face in the way she loved. When he placed his lips to hers, she was soon lost in the strong emotions that flowed between them. When the kiss ended, she buried her face in his broad chest. He had started out as a good friend from another time, but she knew that their love would last a lifetime.

Please Check Out Zoe Matthews' Social Media Sites!!

For the latest information on updates, new releases and sales for Zoe Matthews' books, you can sign up for her newsletter at zoematthewsromances. You will also receive three free books!!!!

Website: zoematthewsromances.com

Email Address: Zoe@zoematthewsromances.com

f facebook.com/zoematthewssr

a amazon.com/Zoe-Matthews/e/B00LDT94U4?ref=sr_ntt_srch_lnk_1&qid=166 6878467&sr=8-1

https://twitter.com/zoematthewssr?lang=en

youtube.com/channel/UCZoprtvNeKOLrije3LJKl9A

BB bookbub.com/authors/zoe-matthews

Also by Zoe Matthews

Have you read these books?

The Orphan Train Romance Series

In the late 1800s, many orphans were sent to different states in the western United States in order to be provided with stable and loving homes. This series features fictitious orphans who traveled to Texas, the families with which they found homes, and the love they found when they were adults.

An Unexpected Family

The Promise of a Family

Anna

Serena

Katrina

Westward Promises

Westward Skies

Orphan Train Romance Series Boxset, Books 1-5

Majestic Mountain Ranch Romance Series

Six siblings come together at their family ranch after their father's death. They work together to convert their ranch into a dude ranch. Along the way, each of them finds true love.

Colorado Dreams

Colorado Secrets

Colorado Destiny

Colorado Dawn

Colorado Skies

Colorado Promises

Colorado Christmas

Majestic Mountain Ranch Series Boxset, Books 1-7

Mail-Order Brides of America Series

After the death of their infant daughter, Mary, Elizabeth and Thomas decide to open their large plantation home to orphan girls who need a second chance. They name their new home "Mary's Home for Girls." Each book features one of these girls, how they came to Mary's Home, and the decision they make as adults to become a mail-order bride. Each book is set in a different state.

Southern Belle, Prequel

Iowa Destiny

Texas Hearts

Montana Legacy

Nebraska Promise

South Dakota Jewel

Mail-Order Brides of America Series, Five Books in One!

Time Travel Romance Series

Written by Zoe Matthews and Jade Jenson, a mother/daughter team

This series is based in modern times, as well as in the 1800s. Nicki and her friends find themselves swept up in the past when Nicki reads an ad in her local newspaper, advertising for a mail-order bride. Curious, she answers the ad and is soon sent back in time to meet Patrick, a man who owns a large ranch deep in the Rocky Mountains, and his siblings. Nicki's friends soon become involved and what happens next changes their lives forever.

Touched by Time

River of Time

Winds of Time

Time Travel Romance Boxset, Books 1-3

Secrets of Time

Changed by Time

Christmas in Time

Time Travel Romance Boxset, Books 1-6

Harvey Girls Romance Series

Written by Zoe Matthews and Evelyn Michaels, a mother/daughter team

Adelia Burke has co-authored books 4 and beyond

Follow a large family of men (and one daughter) who live in Arizona near the Grand Canyon at the beginning of the 1900s. This series is Historical fiction about the Harvey Girls, a true event that was started by a man named Fred Harvey. These women helped shaped the West in their own way, just as much as the men did.

Desert Dreams

Desert Wishes

Desert Bells

Harvey Girls Romance Series Boxset, Books 1-3

Desert Lily

Desert Sky

Millennial Mail-Order Brides Romance Series

Daniel has six grandchildren who refuse to marry and settle down. So he has to take matters into his own hands. He signs each of them up with a dating website and matches them with someone of his choosing. But will his grandchildren cooperate and allow him to be a modern-day matchmaker?

Always and Forever

Now and Forever

A New Love

A Forever Dream

You're My Everything

Lead Me with Your Heart

Millennial Mail-Order Brides Romance Boxset, Books 1-6

Time Travel Guardians Romance Series

It is 2045 and time travel has been proven to be real. But many devices are falling into the wrong hands, so the Time Travel Guardians were born. Their job is to use time travel to find each device before they are discovered by others. As they travel, they each have a fun adventure and discover love.

Under One Sky

When Love Collides

Starlight Dreams